Welcome to part four of ten's a crowd, I hop[e]
first three parts and are familiar with me and
books charts our lives from 1970 onwards. P[a]
beginnings of my new family. I meet my wife
heralds the dawning of a new era.

## 1979;

## Chapter 17. Choosing a career.

The best year of my life so far started with me making a major decision, well not so much made by me, more like made for me. I left school abruptly. It was just after the Christmas holidays, I was in sixth year sitting enough Highers to get me in to Glasgow University, and I fancied trying something in law. My family and I had been through the courts often enough to ignite an interest in me. I was drawn to the fascinating stories of the people you meet in the canteen at the Sherriff Court and milling about at the front entrance waiting to go in and have a stranger decide the direction their lives were about to take. All kinds of human life seemed to be there and it looked enthralling, but alas it wasn't to be, the door closed abruptly on that idea.

I was freezing walking to school, I was well enough wrapped up but there was the bitterest of wind blowing sleet in my face and down the neck of my Parka Jacket. It looked really good the green Parka with the fur hood, but when you are walking into a Scottish wind, the hood bellowed out if you didn't keep your head down, and if you did keep your head down enough, you inevitably walked into things, or people.

"Who is that under there, can you watch where you are bloody going" I recognised the voice but was struggling to get my hood down to see who was berating me. It didn't help that she had a grip of one side of the hood and was pulling me round to try and get a look at me. I struggled free but in doing so inadvertently struck the arm of the woman holding on to my hood. I was only slightly taken aback when I discovered it was Mrs Hunter the deputy headmistress and my former English teacher, I had thought it was her by the whiney voice.

We had never really got on, she preferred silent pupils, the better to hear her own voice but being a McCallister I struggled with the very concept of silence.

1

"Ouch" she screamed, well it sounded like a scream to my ears.

"Now you have hurt my arm, wasn't running into me good enough for you, was that insufficient pain to inflict on me, did you feel a cracked rib needed to be joined by a broken arm to be worthwhile" she said condescension dripping off every word.

"Are your ribs cracked or your arm broken miss, or is that maybe a wee tiny bit of an exaggeration" I asked, sarcasm dripping from my words.

"Don't be insolent Daniel, sixth year or not, prefect or not, I can and will march you to the headmasters office. He has a very dim view of insolence" she said sternly.

"Yes miss, I noticed his dim view, maybe he should get one of those little cloths for cleaning his milk bottle glasses" I said smiling and quickly adding "Only joking miss, it was just an accident I didn't mean to run into you, I was trying to keep my head down it's absolutely freezing out here today, brass monkeys in fact" I smiled again, hoping to charm her. It didn't work, I tried again.

"Will you be ok miss, or would you like to sit on the steps there and I will run and get the nurse, although to be honest miss the only thing that nurse has ever done for me is find some nits. I went to her with a sprained ankle once and she said, "What do you want me to do, x-ray your ankle with my eyes, go to hospital you stupid boy" So unless you've got nits I wouldn't bother miss, do you want to lean on me and I will help you inside" I said, we were about thirty yards from the school gate. I said all of this with another smile and I am sure she wanted to shout at me for longer, but couldn't quite find a reason.

"Go and get on with some learning Daniel, you are in a very obvious need of some" she said dismissing me. She clearly would have liked to make a bigger deal of it, I could feel her glare on my back, even through a thick Parka.

I went straight up to the sixth year common room, there was nobody there, it was only half eight but usually somebody would be in. My first period wasn't until ten o'clock and it was modern studies, a subject I had taken just to fill in my school day, it was mostly about politics, something I had little interest in, I was swithering whether to even bother with the class or bed down under the table in the common room and read a book

2

given to me by one of the English teachers, Of Mice and men, it was called, I had started it the night before and was already engrossed two chapters in.

The bedding down and reading won, the table I lay under was snugly pushed up against a radiator and out of any draughts, I made a pot of tea, presuming that somebody would be in shortly and settled down under the table to read. I lit a cigarette, because that's what I would normally do if I was in my house reading get some tea and light up a fag.

I had only started smoking a few months before. Charlie had burst into my room with a bulging black bin bag and said "Danny, stuff these under your bed or something I'll be back in a minute" I never even looked in them, I knew they were full with something he had nicked, but wasn't that interested, I kicked them under my bed and got back under the quilt and back into the book I was reading. He reappeared after half an hour with another two black bags. "Put these under as well" he said huffing and puffing.

"You put them under, what am I your fuckin butler or something" I said turning my back on him.

"Come on Danny, I'm knackered" he said bending over with hands on hips trying to get his breath back "shove them under your bed before my Ma or Da hear us"

"I canny be bothered with this Charlie, what is all this shit and where did you get it" I asked, getting out of bed and pushing him aside so I could squeeze the bags under my bed. I then took the chance to look into one of them. It was full of cigarettes, Benson & Hedges, Kensitas Club, Silk Cut, Capstan full strength, every brand you could think off and what looked like dozens of packets of Old Holborne and Golden Virginia tobacco.

"Jesus Christ Charlie, have you tanned the paki shop again, poor wee Mr Patel's gonny be greeting all day again, remember the last time you did it, he was inconsolable" I said laughing and putting on what I thought was an Indian voice "I am so good to these people why would they do such a thing Daniel, look at my tick book, look at all those names, why would someone rob a poor old man like me, it's very bad Daniel, it's not a good thing at all is it"

Charlie laughed and said "Aye I know, I nearly gave him the stuff back he was that upset, but then his boy Aakar told me the old bastard doubled up on his insurance claim and was as happy as a pig in shit"

"So was it Mr Patel's is this where all the fags came from" I asked picking up the second bag, and rummaging through it. It was mostly fags as well but they were interspersed with bars of chocolate, Dairy Milk, fry's cream and Aero's mostly.

"No" he said almost recovered from his exertions "It was an ice cream van parked in Lendel place, I noticed it on the way back from Iris's house, it was just sitting at a close asking to be robbed, sheer stupidity if you ask me, who would leave an ice cream parked at a close round here, do they not know that I live here" he said laughing his head off.

I could almost smell the adrenalin off of him, it was always a rush to Charlie, he got high on the act itself not always by what he got, he nicked things as easy as I breathe, just because he could and it always lifted his spirits. I think he thought it was a small victory each time he got away with it, it proved to him that he had outsmarted someone and was cleverer than them just for that moment, Charlie was always smiling or grinning at the best of times. But when he had just lifted something and I had clocked him doing it, he would flash a proud beaming smile at me as if to say, did you see how clever I was there Danny. It was as if he had done a conjuring trick successfully.

"You're gonny go to jail Charlie, and for what?  A packet of fags and a Curly Wurly, you're off your head" I said opening a Mars bar and biting into it as I lay back down. "Did anybody see you" I asked picking my book back up.

"I don't know" he replied "Mrs Wilson in the close was twitching at her curtains, you know what she's like, sits at the window day and night waiting to see somebody fall on their arse, she's an old vulture" He said.

"So you came all the way along paisley road and down the street, somebody else will have seen you, it's ten o'clock at night Charlie and you are running back and forward with black bags full of stuff and you think nobody noticed you, dream on" I said shaking my head, "Get this stuff out of here tonight, I'm not taking the blame for you again, I mean it"

4

He jumped on top of me and kissed the top of my head and ruffled my hair "Don't go shitting yourself Danny Boy, it's some fags and sweeties, I will have them sold before midnight, and in fact I might nick over and see if Mr Patel wants to buy them"

I pushed him off and said "Patel's is shut, it shuts at ten"

He dragged three of the bags out from under the bed and said "Alright joking aside, I will put these bags behind the coal bunker, I don't want you getting the jail, you're too pretty all they lifers would use and abuse you" He carried two of them out and I could hear him stuffing them in the coal bunker cupboard. This was a dark and smelly place, it was obviously full of coal, we got a bag delivered every week by a coal lorry. The guys who brought it up to the house had coal dust ingrained in their skin and hair and the whites of their eyes seemed to glow out at you. The coal wasn't the problem though we also had a cat that liked to shit in the bunker when it couldn't get out. I remember many mornings going to get coal to light the fire in the kitchen and scraping the coal into a coal bucket by hand and picking up soft cat shit by mistake. I can almost still feel it and smell it now, it was gross.

Charlie tied the necks on the two bags and put them up on a top shelf in the bunker cupboard, to keep them free of coal dust and cat shit. He came back to my room for the other two bags and said

"Here" as he looked inside the smaller of the two bags "you can have this bag, there's a few fags and a lot of chocolate in it" and threw the bag back under the bed and picked up the last bag to take it to the coal cupboard. Somebody knocked on the front door just as he stepped into the hall, he looked at me, and I shrugged my shoulders and went towards the door. Charlie gestured for me to wait until he got the third bag put away, the door got knocked again, loudly. Charlie threw the bag into his own room where it landed half under his bed. The door was rattled again louder still, my Da came out of the living room. "Who the fuck is trying to kick the door in" he said to me and looked with suspicion at Charlie, Charlie and I both shrugged, but Charlie opened the door.

There was a huge guy standing their well over six feet and he must have weighed twenty stone, he grabbed Charlie by the front of his shirt and pulled him towards him and shouted in his face "Did you tan my van you wee bastard"

Both me and my Da rushed at him, my Da was quicker, he pushed Charlie out of the way and punched this monster of a man right in the face. I was a wee bit shocked, this guy was huge. Before the guy could recover his equilibrium I heard my Da say, "Gimme that" and take a baseball bat from Charlie's hand, I had seen this bat before it was an aluminium one that John Lawson kept in the boot of his car, Charlie must have nicked it from him. My Da threw the bat behind him into the hall, and turned to the giant at the door and said "I don't need that bat do I big man, because you're gonny just get the fuck away from my door aren't you." My Da looked at Charlie and then back at the stranger and said "And he's been in all night, ok"

The big guy looked at my Da and then at Charlie and me, went to say something and then thought better of it and turned and walked down the stairs. I was amazed, he could probably have battered the three of us. My Da turned to Charlie and slapped him right across the face, hard. Charlie flew half the length of the hall before crashing into the phone table and scattering the phone and the wee money box off it.

My Da went after him again and grabbed him back to his feet, he swung his arm again. I don't know if it would have been a punch or a slap, but I got in between his arm and Charlie's face and said "Hold on a minute Da, you don't even know if he's done anything yet". My Da got a grip of the hair on the back of my head and said "Get in your room Danny" and pushed me towards my room. I bounced back and held his arm again, "No Da, I'm not just letting you batter him for nothing, I'm eighteen da he's seventeen you canny just slap us when you feel like it.

I don't know why I said that, in my eighteen years I could remember my Da hitting me twice and both times I deserved it. When I was a younger teenager my Ma would have to hit me and Charlie every day and without exception we also deserved that. But this was different. In my mind I was a man and so was Charlie, my Da wouldn't just slap Donnie or Dunky like this so he shouldn't hit Charlie either. Maybe he recognised this maybe not but he just pushed Charlie away and said "I am sick of you bringing trouble to this door"

When my Da pushed him Charlie fell onto the phone seat, my Da walked away and Charlie grinned at me, he really could be an idiot, if my Da turned his head and seen that grin he would kill him. He did turn back and went to Charlie's room, he spotted the black bag that was lying half under

6

the bed and stooped to pick it up, as soon as he did this Charlie was up and out the front door on the run. I think he ran down four flights of stairs before my Da even lifted the bag. My Da looked inside the bag and then held it open so that I could see what was in it. I already knew what was in it and could only shrug my shoulders and feign innocence.

He looked me straight in the eye and said "He's gonny get you hurt one day Danny, you canny keep putting yourself in front of him" and I replied "Aye I can Da, and if I didnae you would batter me for not doing it"

My Da lifted the black bag and went into the living room with it, he sat in the chair by the fire and started throwing the contents into the open fire.

"What's the point of that Da" I asked

"We're not having stolen stuff in this house and your brother needs to learn that" he said continuing to feed packs of cigarettes and bars of chocolate into the fire. Paul and David my two youngest brothers were in bed, they would have been heartbroken to see all the bars of chocolate being wasted like that. I decided to go back to bed, if Charlie came back in at all that night then he would have to face my Da's wrath on his own. Just as I was leaving the living room I spotted my Da throwing my Ma some of her brand of fags, Kensitas club, and he also threw her a bar of Cadbury's Fry's Cream, her favourite chocolate, and I am pretty sure he tucked a couple of packs of Old Holborne and a bar of Old Jamaica into his cardigan pocket.

So that was how I started to smoke, the bag Charlie had given me had about twenty packs of cigarettes in it and half a dozen packs of tobacco, and loads of sweets and chocolate. I gave the tobacco to Donnie and shared the chocolate out between Paul and David over the next couple of weeks, every time I gave them something they looked at me with suspicion, the ungrateful wee shits.

As I was saying if you can remember, I had set myself up quite comfortably underneath the desk by the radiator and settled down to read Of Mice and Men and lit up a fag.

"What do you think you are doing boy" Mrs Hunter bellowed.

"No, what do you think you're doing" I asked back at her nonchalantly. "This is the sixth year common room, don't you think you should chap the door before you come in"

"Don't be so insolent boy don't just lie there get on your feet and put that bloody cigarette out" she shouted and I mean shouted.

I did get up and I did put my cigarette out in an ashtray which was on top of the table I had been under. "Calm down Miss, what's all the shouting and bawling for, I don't have a class until the second period, I was just getting warm and having a wee read" I said, reasonably.

"Who do you think you are" she almost screamed at me "This is not your bloody hovel, to lay around smoking in, this is a school, a place you come to learn, not laze about in smoking bloody cigarettes you idiotic boy"

"You should tell that to Mr Jackson Miss, he's never out of the staff room and definitely never without a roll up in his hand. And there's been plenty of times I've seen you with a fag hanging out the corner of your mouth while you're making the tea in there. All you need is a headscarf and you would be a dead ringer for Andy Capp's missus" I said almost laughing, how was I to know she was taking all of this so serious.

She came towards me and raised her hand, I honestly think she was going to slap me. I moved back slightly and put my arm out to block any blow and she fell, I don't know what she tripped over, probably her own feet she was so blazingly mad.

"You pushed me" she screamed like a ten year old lassie. A whiney ten year old lassie as well.

Now I was getting angry "Give yourself fucking peace you stupid self-righteous old hag, you fell over your own fucking feet trying to slap me, what the fuck did you barge in here for anyway have you got no fucking manners, did your Ma never teach to chap the door before entering a room. I could have been doing anything in here for all you know. I could have had a bird in here or something. Now get the fuck out and if you want to come back in chap the fucking door." I said derisively, not the first time I had shouted my mouth off with a high degree of stupidity and it wouldn't be the last.

She was slightly taken aback, no not slightly she was completely taken aback by my outburst. I had turned away from her after I had finished shouting at her, so I didn't see her leave but I heard the door open and close.

I couldn't think for a few minutes, when my blood boils like that, I often take a few minute to calm down. When I did I gathered up my books and put them in the Adidas kit bag I used as a school bag and went to leave. Mr Robertson the PE teacher and rugby coach, barged in and grabbed me by the front of my shirt and pulled me towards the door.

"Hold on a minute sir, let me take my stuff" I said he had pulled me so abruptly I had dropped my bag.

He let me go and pushed me back into the room, "You should be ashamed of yourself boy, how dare you push a defenceless woman old enough to be your mother"

I laughed and said "Is that what the lying old bag told you, how dare you try and convict me before even speaking to me"

He grabbed me again and pulled me towards him, we were almost nose to nose, he had to lean down quite a long way "I should knock you all round this room, you nasty little boy"

I grinned and said "Why don't you try" I said with typically stupid Govan bravado. I shook myself free of him and lifted my bag. Stick your fucking school right up your big fat arse" I said. "And by the way, I know you're a poof, that's the reason you play rugby, all they sweaty men's bodies in the scrum, everybody knows you're a big fat poof" I slammed the door behind me and ran. I don't know if he came after me, I was down the stairs like greased lightning.

So that was then, I had left school. The headmaster wrote to my Da and told him to bring me in, there would obviously be a suspension but that the matter could be resolved. It also included a letter from my guidance teacher telling him that I had great potential and he should endeavour to force my return to school. My ma was really annoyed at me when I said I wasn't going back, I was eighteen and a man I wouldn't be treated like a wean anymore, especially by snooty teachers who thought they were better than me.

Both my Ma and Da tried to talk me out of it but my mind was made up, I went straight into the co-op and got a full time job starting the next Monday. I regret it now I suppose, or at least I regret not seeing what path my life might have taken, but then again I am very happy with the direction it did take so maybe it was fate and meant to be.

I settled in quickly and within a month I was made a supervisor, I think old Mr Wilson was happy to let me get all the younger boys and lassies that came in to do the shelf stacking into order, they were a bit boisterous for him, He rarely came out of wee office in the back shop anymore and when he did it was usually only for a packet of fig rolls. It only took me a couple of weeks to realise that I wasn't cut out to be a supervisor yet.

"Danny, you just can't do that son, that's right out of order" Mr Wilson was saying as he dipped his fig roll into a glass of orange juice. Yuk.

"Who says I canny, where does it say that in the rule book and who wrote the rules anyway" I said.

I had given Isabella McLafferty the task of restacking the shelves in the confectionary aisle. This was a cushy number, which everybody tried to get whenever it needed done. It wasn't unusual for bags of sweets to be burst inside the outer boxes when you opened them, particularly if you weren't careful with the wee box cutter knife you used. It also wasn't unusual for the person doing the confectionary aisle to fill their pockets with the loose sweets and hand them out to anybody that was passing. So not only did you get to stuff your face with chocolate limes and kola kubes but you got to hand them out to your pals as well.

The problem was that a fifteen year old boy, Graham Young, had already started to fill the shelves and when I went up to him and told him Isabella would be finishing it and he should go and check the dog and cat food aisle he clearly wasn't happy about it.

"That's shite" he said, correctly and reasonably, I thought.

"No that's life" I said smiling. "You have been here two weeks, you work part time as a shelf stacker, and I have been here two years, I work full time as a supervisor, look" I said pointing to my badge which said, Supervisor. "So go and dig out the boxes of Pedigree Chum and Kit-e-Kat and get on with it pal"

"It's still shite" He replied and again he was probably right "You are only shifting Isabella on to this because you fancy her and everybody knows it." He accused.

"And?" I asked him quizzically "What's your point, of course I fancy her have you seen her, lovely looking and boobs like melons, do you no fancy her? Or are you saying I should leave you here and then everybody will think I fancy you instead?"

He went beetroot red and stammered "I never meant that, are you a poof or something"

"Wouldn't you like to know sweetheart" I answered, "Now go and get the pet food aisle done, run along be a good boy"

Mr Wilson answered me "I write the rules and I'm telling you. You can't give easy jobs to the lassies you fancy and hard jobs to the boys you don't like"

"How no?" I asked bewildered by his statement "What's the point of being a supervisor then it's certainly no the four pence an hour extra wages, so what is it?"

He laughed and said "No, it's not the extra money, let me rephrase it, if you do want to give the easy jobs to wee stunners like Isabella you need to be a bit more crafty a bit more subtle, do you know what that means"

"I know what it means Mr Wilson, but I live in Cessnock which is practically Govan, we don't really do subtle in Govan, do you know what I mean." I said grinning.

"Aye I know what you mean Danny" he said and chuckled "But you still canny tell wee boys like Graham that you are taking him off one job and on to another because you are trying to get your hands up a lassies jumper."

I interrupted him "I've had my hands up her jumper, it's my hands down her pants I'm after now"

He exploded in laughter "Get out and sort it out Danny, and don't have that wee boy Graham coming in complaining to me again"

That I could do. "Graham, come on with me son, I've got a job for you" I said walking through the warehouse towards the back door. He followed and stood beside me as I pointed to the giant skip in the back yard.

"See that skip" I asked, he nodded.

"See that cardboard and crap all around that fence" I asked pointing at piles of wet cardboard and litter stuck to the chain link fence around the yard. "Get it all lifted and into that skip and I need it done before you finish for the day"

"It's raining" he said.

"Well done" I said "If we ever need a weatherman in the Govan co-op, I will put your name forward, but right now we need somebody to tidy the yard up, and that somebody is you, and you can be proud of yourself because I think you work so hard and since this is a difficult job which only the hardest workers can do, then I am pleased to tell you that it's your permanent job now, so every night when you come in you can come straight out here and get started, well done, consider it a promotion"

I walked away "Before you start, go and have your tea break, and get a pair of thick gloves from the store cupboard, there's always some rats living round the bottom of that fence especially near the corner of the building, and you don't want them biting you and watch you don't pick up anything they have pissed or shit on with your bare hands because they spread really awful diseases. Well that's what I was told by blind Willie, the old alky that sits at Govan cross."

About half an hour later Mr Wilson asked me what I had done with Graham. Apparently he went in for his tea break and that was the last anybody had seen of him. When he never turned up over the next three days, Mr Wilson posted his outstanding wages to him. Isabella left about two weeks later, she got a part time job in Marks and Spencer's a nice step up from the Govan co-op. I never did get my hand up her jumper, I was just showing off to Mr Wilson, but at least it got his old heart going a bit.

I only lasted another four weeks in the co-op, it was far too boring. Mr Wilson had tried to talk me out of it, he told me he was retiring in two years and that if I waited until the end of this year he would make me up to assistant manager and I would have the chance to become store manager when he retired.

"I don't think so Mr Wilson, I'm only eighteen, when you retire I will only be twenty, who would give a manager's job to a wee boy of twenty?" I asked him as we sat in his wee office, drinking coffee and eating Jaffa cakes that had come from a pack I accidentally on purpose ripped open when I clumsily cut the carton open.

"You are only a young boy Danny, but you pick everything up like lightening. Look at yesterday, you did all the vegetable ordering and all the dairy ordering. I only showed you how to do those three days ago, and now you are doing it yourself. Most of the time now I canny be bothered with this I'm ready to retire just now, I would if I could. If you hang about you would probably be running this place in six months and I can just sit in this back office and read my Agatha Christie's. I can teach you all you need to know about groceries" He laughed and said "And you can teach me about getting my hands up the jumpers of lassies like Isabella"

"Aye, right and then who would give you the kiss of life, not me pal" I laughed with him.

It was a good offer, old Mr Wilson was one of the good guys. He was strict enough when he needed to be, but he knew it was only a job of work, it wasn't life and death. He wasn't like some managers, so puffed up with his own importance that he never seen the lives of the people he worked with. It was common to find one or two of the lassies sitting down in his office occasionally doing some paperwork, instead of being on the shop floor or at the tills. We usually found out later that they had been emotional about something or other, fell out with a boyfriend or a late period or a difficult period, and he had spotted their discomfort and let them sit in the nice quiet office, away from greeting weans and crabbit pensioners.

He would also often be seen handing out the occasional fiver or tenner when somebody was a bit skint, he also had a wee private tick book for a couple of the older woman on the tills, the one's with men that visited the bookies and the pub with their wage packet before they went home. The amazing thing was that in maybe eighteen months I had been there I had never seen any of the women take advantage of his nature. There were two older women in particular on the tills, Agnes and Ina. Both of them were ages with my Ma, and both of them were worldly wise, Glasgow style. They knew what was what, who was who and why you should and why you shouldn't.

They were like bodyguards to him, if anybody wanted anything from him, they would interrogate them first. They knew before I did and probably before he did that Mr Wilson had taken a shine to me and seen me as a possible successor to his wee kingdom of Govan. And it was a kingdom, it wasn't just the staff he looked and after and kept on the right path, I seen him with shoplifters, being hard as nails or soft as butter.

"Danny, did you see that?" he asked. Nodding towards an old woman in what looked like an old grey army coat four sizes too big for her. It was a week before Christmas.

"What do you want me to say" I asked "If you mean did I see her putting that wee frozen chicken inside her coat, then no I didn't, officially"

"That's not how it works Danny, this isn't your shop or my shop. We can't get to decide who gets to steal from it and who doesn't. It might not be nice but we do have a job to do." He looked at me with some sympathy and said "Go outside when she leaves the shop, bring her back in and through to my office"

I stood outside and watched her progress through the tills. I stared hard at her hoping she would get the message and take the chicken it and pay for it. She didn't.

"Excuse me Mrs, you will need to come back into the shop, you were seen taking some things that you haven't paid for and the manager wants a word about it" I said placing my hand on her elbow.

She looked at me with a sly grin, and gave a coquettish giggle as if she was some young lady of the manor and had been caught without a handkerchief.

"Hello Danny, how are you son" she said "And how is your Dorothy, is she liking it in Redcar, that was a terrible thing with her we wean, it fair broke my heart so it did. I stood there mouth agape. I thought I recognised the old biddy, and she had confirmed my suspicions

"Shut your mouth son, you will catch flies. I'm Tony's Granny, Philomena, we met at Dorothy and Tony's wedding.  Do you not mind me I sat at the top table, after I pointed how terrible ignorant they had been, that is."

I laughed out loud, if I had been American I would have slapped my knee. I still said nothing, she was covering all the angles.

"Right away you go back in and tell that nice Mr Wilson that I gave you the slip, tell him you spotted somebody else up to no good and I must have went through the tills without you seeing me" she said grinning "Or tell him I outran you and got on a bus" she cackled like an old hen.

I lifted my eye brows and looked towards the till area inside the store. She followed my gaze and seen Mr Wilson looking at us. I shook my head at him letting him know I wasn't bringing her back in. He came out of the store and said. "You need to come to my office Madam" and took her firmly by the arm.  She followed him in, but not without first giving me a withering look that told me not only was I a disappointment to my family but a traitor to the working class people of Govan, well that's what it said to me.

"Philomena Murphy, as I live and breathe" Mr Wilson said smiling "I thought you had given this lark up, after the last time" I stood behind him as he sat at his desk and Tony's granny sat opposite him.

"Gave what up" she asked full of innocence and pretend confusion.

"Gave up thieving" Mr Wilson said firmly.

"Thieving, thieving how dare you John, I went to school with you big sister, she would be ashamed of you, calling a poor old wee woman a thief with no evidence at all, it's disgraceful so it is"

"Danny go and take the frozen chicken out of her coat before it defrosts and she's sitting in a puddle of water" Mr Wilson said to me.

Mrs Murphy cackled and said "It widnae be the first time I was sitting in a puddle of water, if you know what I mean son" she looked at me full of mischief "In fact it widnae even be the first time the day" and she went off into a raucous bout of laughter at her own joke which ended with a coughing fit and her going red in the face. I bolted round the desk and started slapping her on the back, she stood up and slapped me on the back of the head and continued her coughing. When she eventually stopped she tried to slap me again.

"What are you doing, you stupid wee article you almost killed me" she spluttered.

"I was only slapping your back to help you Mrs Murphy" I said chastened and scared I had done her some damage"

"Aye but every time you slapped me this was banging right into my ribs and stopping my breath you halfwit" she said, extracting a three and a half pound frozen chicken from an inside pocket off her huge coat.

Both Mr Wilson and I laughed as it thumped down onto the desk in front of her. "Is there anything else in there, Philomena, tell me the truth you don't want me to send Danny in to rummage through them big pockets now, do you" Mr Wilson said with high amusement at her predicament.

"Oh and wouldn't that be a fine thing" she said "Myself telephoning Dorothy to tell her that her young brother makes a living interfering with defenceless old woman"

"You're as about defenceless as the red army" I said to her laughing "And you've got one of their coats on as well by the looks of it."

She emptied her pockets of a couple of tins of boiled ham, two packets of fresh corned beef, and a Fray Bentos steak and kidney pie"

When I looked at the last item with raised eyebrows "Boxing day" was all she said.

Mr Wilson berated her for a few minutes about what a bad example she was setting to younger people and how she should be ashamed of herself for probably encouraging her grandchildren into crime, but he wasn't going to take it further and get the police. She was barred from the shop until after the New Year, because we were too busy to be watching out for her, He threatened her with the police the next time we had any bother with her at all, "Even a jar of sardine paste and its Cornton Vale for you" he said. It didn't help when I had butted in and told him that having met most of her grandchildren it was probably them that were encouraging her into a life of crime.

We gave her a cup of tea and a wee biscuit and I got one of the girl shelf stackers to walk her round to the Wine Alley, an area in Govan, where she lived. It was a Saturday afternoon so I finished at six, as I was leaving Mr Wilson gave me a shout and said "Danny take this with you" he handed me a co-op carrier bag which was so full it was tearing the handles, I repacked it in a box and asked" What's this for"

"Take it to Mrs Murphy" he whispered and winked at me, It was all the things she had tried to nick as well as a Birds fruit trifle a Christmas pudding and a box of mince pies" I smiled at him and all he said was "Beat it, get out of my sight before I change my mind"

When I took it to her house, bear in mind I had to walk half a mile with it on my shoulder, her reaction was much as I expected.

"I hope that's not the same Chicken Danny son, it was starting to defrost earlier on, are you trying to poison me, and what's that a Christmas Pudding and no brandy sauce, that's going to be a bit dry is it no. And I canny stand mince pies, take them home for your Ma. It looks like a cemetery for dead flies when you put your fork into one of them." She guided me firmly towards the door with her hand in my back and the box of mince pies in my hand.

I opened the door and she virtually pushed me over the doorstep. Before I could get away she dragged me back by the arm and kissed me on the cheek. "For a wee proddy dog, you're not beyond redemption son" She gave my cheek a wee tug with her fingers  which she probably intended to be affectionate but was actually sore, or maybe it was meant to be sore and I took it as affectionate.

So all in all I suppose I could have done worse than stay at the co-op, Mr Wilson really was one of the good guys and I had learned a lot from him and he still had a lot to teach me and I still had plenty to learn, not just about the co-op, about everything. But incidents like the one with Mrs Murphy or the dalliance with Isabella and her sultry Italian eyes, were too few and too far between. Working at the co-op was ninety nine per cent putting things on shelves and one per cent fun. I wanted it the other way round.

I started scanning the papers for a new job and decided to try and be a bit more upmarket in my search because I had good qualifications and should try to use them, so I was on the hunt for a job in an office. Mainly because whenever my Ma talked about me or to me about my finding a job she seemed to think this was a pinnacle worth aspiring to. "A job in an office" was a big deal to her.

So I went for interviews as an office junior in law offices, everybody was too up themselves for my liking, In a surveyors office, I could have went for that, but when the interviewer said I might want to soften my Glasgow accent, I called him a prick and walked out. The job I ended up with was an apprentice quality control engineer in a plastics factory in Hillington Industrial estate. It wasn't directly an office job, but it was a trade.

The main reason I took it was because it included a two year engineering course at Cardonald College on a day release basis. And that could only be good in the long run. My Da surprised me because he was actually as proud as punch when I got that job, if you asked him his preference between lawyers and engineers, he would plump for an engineer.

I really enjoyed this job, it was a plastics factory where they made all manner of things. From plastic cups with lids for babies to drink out of with wee baby elephants printed on the side, a pale blue for boys and an insipid pink for girls, to intricate plastic widgets which were part of the trigger device for land mines. The parts were all moulded on huge machines which worked by melting plastic pellets and then pressing them into the shapes that were needed. This was a job carried out by men only, it was heavy sweaty work. In the mould room the guys were stripped down to shorts and a pair of sandshoes, they all had an allowance of eight glass bottles of Irn Bru or Strike Cola per day, Because they lost a significant amount of fluids doing what they did.

When the parts came out of these huge machines, it was my job to inspect them and either pass them through to the finishing hall or reject them. Rejected batches could cost somebody ten or twenty quid off their weekly bonus, so it was a common occurrence for some of these guys to argue the point with me and try to get me to pass defective batches. I was regularly offered bribes to switch tags on rejected batches so that someone other than the person offering the bribe would get the blame for shoddy work, I resisted the temptation, knowing that it would be my job on the line if I gave in. I actually did it once and once only, because the operator who's work I was about to reject was being picked on by the mould room foreman, Jack Bryson, who wanted him sacked so he could get his cousin a job.

Jack deliberately gave this guy a dodgy batch of pellets and as a result the plastic wing mirror cases he made were a disaster. I knew what was going on because there had been a lot of whispering about what Jack was doing and why he was doing it. When the bucket of parts came to me for inspection, I didn't even have to take any samples out and look at them. There was supposed to be four hundred wing mirror cases in the bucket, in fact there were probably thirty or forty and a huge bundle of scrap plastic. I don't know why, it was really nothing to do with me, but I swapped the tag on this bucket for the tag on the next bucket, which by fate or coincidence belonged to a mate of the foreman.

I was sitting in the canteen having my lunch, at a table with nine women. The women in this factory all worked in the finishing hall. After I passed batches from the moulding room, they were taken to the finishing hall where there were six long tables which each held fifty or so women who finished the products by hand. Mostly what they did was file away rough edges left by the moulds and packed the components into boxes awaiting shipment.

Jack Bryson came over to the table and whispered "Have you got a minute wee man" and tugged at the collar of my white warehouse coat. Engineers and managers wore white warehouse coats, so they carried some authority but since I was a first year apprentice that had only been there less than a month, in my case any authority was dubious.

"What for" I asked, putting half of my steak pie onto a roll and munching on it.

"Because I want a word in your shell like wee man, that's why, so move it" he said this time pulling the collar of my coat quite roughly.

One of the women at the table said "Leave him alone Jack he's only a wee boy"

I said "Aye leave the wee boy alone Jack, or he might kick you in the stones." Pulling his hand off my collar and glaring at him.

Jack Bryson was probably mid-thirties and weighed nearly double what I did. His mate, whose tag I had swapped was slightly younger, slightly lighter and much uglier. His three front teeth were missing and when he opened his mouth to laugh at me for threatening his pal, he looked like a hillbilly.

"What are you laughing at Jeremiah Clampett" I said to him. The women at the table were obviously fans of the TV show The Beverly Hillbillies, because they all burst out laughing. I realised I was getting in a bit deep, it's one thing to argue with these guys it's a different thing entirely to have women laughing at them. So in an effort to calm it down before it got nasty, I finished my roll and steak pie and followed Jack to the table they were sat at.

"What's the problem" I asked in a reasonably friendly manner as I sat down.

Jack Bryson answered just as another one of his pals sat down at the table, "The problem's all yours wee man, you must have swapped Stewarts bucket for that wee shite Simmy's bucket, and that's upset my plans. I need him out the door so I can get my wee cousin in, and you got in my way. So when you're finished your dinner wee man, go upstairs and put right the mistake you made and we will say no more about it" he said in a condescending tone, no doubt intended to leave me in no doubt who was the boss.

"My lunch" I said.

"What about your fucking lunch" toothless Stewart asked.

"This is my lunch, not my dinner, you'se lot have got no class, in fact you'se are quite uneducated. And by the way Jack, I never made any mistake with Jeremiah's bucket, the only mistake is you thinking that I'm a dickhead, newsflash for you, I'm no" I said with a grin and left the canteen.

I went straight to the quality control manager, my boss, and told him I was getting a bit of grief from Jack Bryson and asked how I should handle it. He more or less told me that anything I did with Bryson he would back me up, because in his words "He's an idiot that needs taking down a peg or two"

I went back to the moulding room to continue doing my job. Jack Bryson and both of his ugly pals went out of their way to approach me and all three of them said basically the same thing to me. Bryson himself was probably the most eloquent.

"You're not always going to be in here with a white coat on you wee prick, you need to stand at the number fifty four bus stop on with your wee green parka on at half past five, see you there then wee man and we can show you how uneducated we really are."

I used the same sardonic smile to respond to all three, I am sure none of them could see my legs shaking nervously as I was behind a table which was bedecked with plastic components. I had a tea break at three o'clock, I used it to phone home, and the only person in the house was Paul. I didn't want to drag him into it, but needs must. I told him three guys were going to jump me when I got out of work and to go and find Charlie and tell him to meet me at the bus stop outside my work.

I had no way of knowing if Paul could find Charlie and no way of knowing whether Charlie would take it seriously or laugh it off. I spent the next couple of hours in behind the inspection table, because as long as I was in there, nobody could sneak up behind me. I didn't even go to the toilet all afternoon, just in case.

Half past five arrived eventually and when the hooter went for work to finish, I made my way to the office rapidly, grabbed my jacket and bolted away as quick as I could. I knew my three potential protagonists would need to get dressed before they could follow me. It was the end of March and the rain was pouring down outside, so it was unlikely they would be running out in their shorts. But they had anticipated what I would do and they were already dressed by the time I got out of the building they were right behind me.

I looked around for Charlie, nothing. I had to make a decision, run or nonchalantly go and stand at the bus stop and bluff it out. There were about four hundred people coming out of our factory with maybe another couple of thousand from surrounding factories. Talking of which I spotted one of the workers from the Rowat's the beetroot factory coming towards me and I called out to her.

"Darlene" I shouted "How are you getting home, are you getting the bus" Darlene had moved up to Pollokshields some months before but she still worked at Rowat's and normally John Lawson came and got her.

Two things happened as I shouted on Darlene. Jack Bryson and his two pals bundled into me and pushed me into the bus shelter and started throwing punches. One or two connected, I had both arms up protecting my head and I turned myself into the corner of the shelter and crouched down, so that all that was exposed to their punches was my back. I had it mind to bolt as soon as I had half a chance. But the other thing that happened at just about the same time was a screeching of tyres. I couldn't look up to see whether it was a bus knocking somebody down or just a van trying to avoid the three stooges that were after me or maybe even Darlene. After a few seconds of not being hit I dared to look up and seen Charlie swinging a baseball bat about and whacking both Jack Bryson and toothless Stewart several times about the back and the arms.

John Lawson had the third guy pinned up against the wall of the bus shelter, repeatedly punching him in the face. Darlene ran across the road causing more traffic to screech, she ran towards Charlie I assumed she was going to try and stop Charlie swinging the bat, she didn't she went straight past him and started throwing punches at toothless Stewart. By this time he was finished fighting anyway His arms were down by his sides and he wasn't able to defend himself against her onslaught. It was all over in minutes, I dragged Charlie away from Jack Bryson, who was rolled in a ball in the corner of the bus shelter.

"Stop Charlie, that's enough" I said, I pulled him back and saw anger, real anger in his eyes.

"No it isnae Danny, three of them onto one of you, I'm going to put this bastard in a wheelchair, Jack Bryson starting sobbing, I pulled Charlie well away , put one hand on each side of his head and pulled him close looking into his eyes and told him "Leave it, Charlie, he's done, finished kaput."

Charlie came out of rage induced trance and we both then pulled Darlene away from toothless Stewart and John Lawson let the third guy slump to the ground. John turned to me and asked "Do you need a lift home Danny or are you going on the bus with some of they birds."

I looked round, there was a bunch of about eight or nine lassies that I recognised from the finishing hall in my work, all standing at the same bus stop, and all looking straight at me. Much to Lawson's surprise I chose the lift home. Bryson and his pals never bothered me again as long as I worked there.

### Chapter 18. The most beautiful girl in the world.

One of the best things about working at that factory was the finishing hall, three hundred women and about a third of them were aged between sixteen and twenty, if I couldn't find a girlfriend amongst that lot, there was definitely something wrong with me. The problem I had though manifested itself quite quickly, there were too many lassies and only one of me. What I mean was, the factory was split into three main areas, the moulding room and warehouse, the finishing hall and the offices.

The guys from the moulding room only really mixed with the women from the finishing hall at tea breaks or lunch time. Even then most of the guys ate at their machines because by the time they got washed and put clothes on to go to the canteen, their lunch break was nearly up, even more so with their fifteen minute tea breaks. I on the other hand spent one week inspecting the parts coming from the moulding presses and the following week inspecting the finished products coming out of the finishing hall, and then swapped over every week after that. So I spent one week every fortnight inspecting goods in the finishing hall.

So, where the guys in the moulding room used to bribe me or threaten me, the lassies in the finishing hall had different ways to try and get me to help them make their bonuses. Nothing terrible, it wasn't like that. But some of them fluttered their eyelashes that much I'm surprised they didn't take off like a helicopter. Other took any opportunity to squeeze past me when I was standing at an inspection table, if there was loads of room on the other side of the table they would still choose to squeeze past me on my side of the table, rubbing all their wobbly bits on me as they did. And that was just the over forties. I wasn't complaining you understand, well most of the time I wasn't.

The younger lassies, the ones I would be interested in, used to leave their names and phone numbers in inspection trays and then smile at me when I found the bit of paper and looked up to see who had left it. That was my big problem you see, before I could ever get round to asking one of them out, another one would leave me their number. So I was like a four year old wean in Woolworths, I was stood staring at the pick and mix and couldn't make my mind up what sweetie I wanted. When I mentioned this one night to Darlene and John Lawson, John said "Well just grab a handful of sweeties and keep trying them to you find one you like" Darlene punched him in the face and called him a philatelist. I think she meant philanderer, and only because she had heard somebody say that on Dallas or Crossroads or something.

I laughed and said to John "Aye you're probably right when I go into to work tomorrow, I'll make a start and ask some of the pretty ones if they fancy a night out"

He answered "Are you stupid, you don't ask the pretty ones out. Their too much like hard work, ask the ugly ones out. Their so desperate they put out on the first night, and when you've finished with the ugly ones then start on the older ones, because their just as grateful as the ugly ones and eventually work your way round to the pretty ones."

Darlene punched him again, but this time she got her insult correct "Arsehole" she said. She then shouted at him for a few minutes but actually started smooching with him when he explained that she hadn't let him finish, that what he was going to tell me was you only go after the really really pretty girl when you want to marry her. She swallowed that, I mean I know Darlene's an eejit but come on hen get a grip.

I did ask one of the girls out, Maureen her name was, she wasn't ugly or old, she was pretty enough, but I asked her out because she was a good laugh, we seemed to share a sense of humour and she never once put her phone number in an inspection tray or tried to get me to pass any dodgy work.

I never actually went out with Maureen at all. I had arranged to go out to the pictures with her on Sunday night. We agreed to meet outside Boots on the corner of Argyle Street and walk up to the Odeon on Renfield Street. But something happened on Friday night that meant I never met up with Maureen.

I finished at four on Friday, my usual routine was straight home and into the bath. Send Paul to get me a sausage supper, I always gave him a pound. A sausage supper was fifty pence and he got to keep the change. Sit at the kitchen table eat my sausage supper, sort out my wages give my Ma twenty quid dig money. Stick a tenner under my bedside lamp and stick whatever I had left in my pocket for weekend drinking money. Usually about eighteen to twenty quid, lager was less than fifty pence a pint so it was game on.

This particular Friday I had no plans, I would usually go to three or four pubs and see if I could find Donnie, Dunky or Charlie, have a game of darts or pool with them and see what mates of mine were hanging about in the same pubs and grab a couple of them and head into shuffles in the city centre. Where we would try and pull. Some weeks were good some weren't, c'est la vie.

I was sauntering down the Paisley road west in my brand new fawn corduroy dungarees, well brand new to me. I had bought them off one of Charlie's mates for a fiver, and I thought I looked the bee's knees. The only problem was that to have a pee you had to unbutton all the way down one side, because there was no zip at the front. When I pointed this out to Smiddy, Charlie's pal that I had bought them from, he agreed and that's why he only took a fiver for them. Charlie laughed and said they were probably women's dungarees and Smiddy only paid two quid for them up the Barra's anyway. Smiddy held me back from punching Charlie.

I looked in our usual haunts, I tried Fergie's bar first. This was quite a trendy pub at the time it was owned by Alex Ferguson, the same Alex Ferguson that became the Manchester United manager. None of my brothers and none of my mates were in that night the same thing happened at the Old Toll Bar, The Quaich and Jim Baxter's. I eventually found Donnie standing in the Viceroy with a couple of his old school pals the McNulty brothers Andy and Willie. I don't know why he drank in that pub it was an old man's pub and as for his two mates, there were a few times they had bolted when the chips were down so I don't know why he drank with them either. I had a pint with him asked him if he had seen Dunky or Charlie and he told me that Dunky was meeting a lassie in the Fountain bar but he was sure Charlie was away down the Gorbals to see Iris. Donnie still seen me as a schoolboy and was delighted to be able to take the piss out of me because of my Dungarees. Or my our Willie trousers as he called them. The McNulty's joined in the fun. I let it go, I didn't want to embarrass Donnie by starting a fight with his two old pals.

So I made my way back down the Paisley road, popping my head into The Wallace Bar, the Red Lion and the Grapes. I was going to look in the Stanley Bar where all the Celtic supporters drunk to see if Charlie was in there he sometimes drunk in there, but with Donnie saying Charlie was in the Gorbals I didn't bother. Dunky was in the fountain, but he was in the bar and steaming, it was only seven o'clock. I spotted Searcher and big Bobby in the bar and asked them when they were leaving, they said shortly they hadn't even been home from work yet.

They agreed to walk Dunky along the road and see that he got up the stair safe enough, I bought them a pint and then watched the practically carry Dunky out, they said they would probably be back down at about nine if I was still about we could have a drink. But to be honest I wanted to go to the dancing and as searcher couldn'y dance and Bobby just shouldn'y dance, I was probably going in on my own. Which most of the time was alright but sometimes could be a bit mental if it was a full moon, there were a lot of head cases in Glasgow city centre, there still are.


So there I was all dressed up and nowhere to go, so I nicked into the lounge just to see what I could see before I headed into the town. And what I saw was the most beautiful girl in the world. I was stunned. She was probably the same height as me, she had on a blue skirt and a white low cut top. She had blonde hair and green eyes. She had the high cheekbones that made Cleopatra so beautiful. I stared at her. Then I stared at her. And then I stared at her again.

I was half in and half out of the door. Somebody barged into my back and said. "Are you coming in or going out Danny for fuck sake, make your mind up son" It was one of Donnie's mate's, presumably doing the same as me, trawling the pubs until he found his pals.

"Have you seen Donnie or the McNulty's" he asked me. He then grabbed me by the back of the neck and turned me around and asked me again. "Viceroy" I said, straining to turn my head back round to the vision of loveliness that had my attention. He laughed and said "Shut your mouth Danny, you could catch flies in there son, out of your league wee man, well out of your league" he said patting me on my head and laughing as he went.

I spotted who this girl, this woman, this beauty, was sitting with, it was Gordon Differ, he was known as Gordon Different because he was a bit odd. I felt a surge of dislike for him, there was no way she could be actually with him, it must be his sister or cousin or something. He was an ugly bastard, with a big nose and a big chin and a big stupid head, why would she have found him when I was out there waiting for her. I had never felt jealousy before and didn't recognise it.

I joined them at their table, there were another couple of boys at the table that I vaguely knew, they were friends of different.

"How's it going different" I asked, not at all interested but I had to say something to get the ball rolling.

Before he could even answer I asked "And who's this then" I was pointing at the girl, the vision of loveliness and beauty, I wasn't even looking at him, when I asked, I was staring at her.

"That's my bird, Patricia" he said. The girl, the beautiful girl, cast a withering glance of dislike at him behind his back, a glance that put joy in my heart. "Well not really my bird this is our first night out together" he said.

"And obviously your last you halfwit" I thought, and smiled at Patricia she read my smile and smiled back. Get in there.

I had known different since I moved to Cessnock so that would be about eight years, I had never spoken more than six words in a row to him. I spent most of that evening sitting at his table with him, Patricia and his friends. I was at the bar getting a drink when I felt a presence at my elbow. It was Patricia fumbling in her bag looking for something. I smiled at her and asked her what she was looking for "My purse" she said. She had long blonde hair well down past her shoulders, beautiful straight blonde hair, as she fumbled for her purse her hair hid her face from me.

I looked at her again and lifted her chin so she was looking at me and I could see her beauty, drink it in. "What for" I eventually asked.

"Gordon says it's my round, he got the last one and it's my turn" she said again casting a withering glance at him.

"Put your purse away hen, I'll get you a drink, never mind him he's an eejit, what are you doing going out with a tube like him anyway, if you don't mind me asking" I said to her, moving in front of her so she was half hidden from him and able to answer without him overhearing her.

"My Ma knows his Ma and, well I don't really know how it happened, but somehow we agreed to meet in here tonight and that was that. It won't happen again" she said.

I looked at her and saw something in her eyes that looked familiar, I knew her, I knew I had seen those eyes before, I couldn't think where from but there was something nagging at me a memory or a memory of a memory, something, just a feeling.

So I bought her a drink and said I hoped I would bump into her again, she shrugged her shoulders nonchalantly. I could have taken that shrug as indifference, perhaps I would have seen indifference in her eyes had I been looking in her eyes but I wasn't, I was looking at the effect that shrug of her shoulders had as it rippled down her body. By the time I did look up again and into her eyes, I was already in love.

She actually left the pub before I did, a friend of hers Sally McFadyen came looking for her at about ten o'clock and they left together, she didn't even say goodbye to Gordon, she did give me the most casual of smiles as she left, and whispered something to Sally, who immediately looked back at me and appraised me completely with one glance. She then grabbed Patricia by the elbow and they exited giggling. I knew of Sally, I didn't actually know her but I could find her if I had to, so that was good, that was absolutely fine and dandy, because if I could find her I could find the beautiful Patricia, and since Patricia had left without dropping a glass slipper, I needed to be able to find her some other way.

Gordon eventually noticed that she wasn't there anymore and asked me if I had seen where she had went. I told him she had left a while back with one of her pals, she had actually just left but I didn't want him chasing after her.

"Good" he said "She was a stuck up wee cow, I don't know why though, because she's a wee tramp. I must have had to ask her four times if she was getting a round in, and I don't think she did. I doubt if she even had any money on her."

I was still thinking of her, in particular her perfect body, her perfect smile her perfect cheekbones her perfect eyes. So I forgot to knock his teeth down his throat for talking about my future wife like that, lucky boy Gordon, lucky boy.

I went into the Fountain bar again on Saturday night, hoping to see her again. I didn't but I found out from one of Gordon's pals that she was staying with her sister in Lambhill Street. Which was only a five minute walk away, so I decided to casually stroll past and see if I could see her, The moment I stepped out of the door of the bar, I spotted Sally, her friend across the other side of the road.

I stepped onto the road oblivious to any traffic and determined to catch up with Sally, so it was a bit of a shock when the taxi hit me. It was a glancing blow, it spun me round and I fell backwards onto the pavement outside the Fountain. I landed on my arse, right on the bone at the top of my arse and it was sore. Sally came across to me and asked "Did you get knocked down by that taxi there?"

"No, that's how I stop them, most people just put their hand out, but I throw myself it them, while their still moving" I said sarcastically.

She looked at me quizzically. "Of course it knocked me down, don't be so stupid" I said, rubbing my sore bum, and showing my usual charm.

"I'm stupid?" she asked "Who's standing outside the Fountain rubbing their sore arse? I'll give you a clue it's one of us, I'll give you another clue, it's not me" she said and walked away head held high.

"Hoy wait a minute Sally, come here, it was you I was running across the road to see so in a way it was your fault" I said catching up with her and putting my arm round her shoulder.

"Get your hands off me, don't touch what you canny afford." She said haughtily pushing my arm off her shoulders and walking on.

I caught up with her again and again I put my arm round her shoulder and hugged her a little, "Don't get all snooty on me Sally, I just wanted a word about your gorgeous wee blonde pal from last night" I said laying it on thick.

She smiled and said "Oh Patricia, you mean. I recognise you now, you were the dope in the pub with your tongue hanging out, and aye Patricia mentioned you to me when we were leaving. Look at that eejit in his sister's dungarees with his tongue hanging out. She's out of your league pal, if you canny afford me you definitely canny afford her." She said with some amused venom.

"Sally, baby. I know you're only trying to wind me up. I could tell she fancied me. In fact I could tell how much you both fancied me, but she saw me first." I said pulling her closer with my arm round her shoulders in a friendly way and raising my eyebrows.

"Patter merchant" she said and pushed me away again "I'm just going round to her sisters, come on with me if you must" she said, smiling. I got the message that meant that Patricia had been talking to Sally and probably was interested, because if she wasn't Sally would have told me to beat it. In fact with the look in her eyes I think Sally fancied me as well, but then I always thought any lassie that didn't punch me in the face, fancied me.

"No, I won't come round I was just going into the Fountain, so tell her she can come round to the pub and I will get her a drink" I said walking backwards towards the pub,  for some reason I wanted her to come to me, it seemed important.

"You were coming out of the Fountain, no into it, that's how you got knocked down with the taxi, ya eejit" she said looking slightly bewildered at my reluctance to go with her. She gave me a puzzled look and strolled away, when she got to the next corner she gave a slight backward glance with a cheeky wee smile attached.

It was almost half past nine, nearly two hours later before Sally popped her head in the lounge door of the Fountain and shouted "Danny boy, your princess is here" I casually gave it about two minutes I didn't want to appear over eager, before I went outside. They were already a couple of hundred yards away. I ran after them no longer bothered about the over eager thing.

Wait up, where are you'se going" I called out to them as I made up the ground.

"We're not standing outside a pub door waiting for you that's what we're no doing" Sally said, linking an arm with Patricia and pulling her forward with her. If anything she was even more beautiful than the night before and I felt something stir inside me. It was like butterflies, a nervousness I had never experienced. I felt my face go slightly red and my heart beat faster.

I caught up with them and walked beside them I stayed on Sally's left hand side with Patricia on her right. I didn't want to get too close in case I crowded her"

"What do you want" Patricia asked looking directly at me. Could I tell her? Could I actually say the words, I want you, I have never wanted anything or anyone more than I want you, ever.

She cut through my hesitation "You told sally to bring me round to the pub, what for? What did you want?" I didn't know how to respond I was tongue tied, so naturally I blurted out nonsense.

"I wanted to know if I could walk you home" I said ignorant of the stupidity of it.

"How stupit are you" Sally asked pushing me in the chest "She was home, she didnae need walking home, she was already in her house when I went to get her for you, Then she took two hours putting her make up on, so that she can walk for five minutes and you can walk her back to where she started, you really are a complete eejit. Come on Patricia, let's go, Betty said she's going to a party, we can go with her" Betty, I later found out was Patricia's sister.

Patricia looked at me and said "Alright then, come on walk me home" Sally looked at her and said "Both of you are as stupid as each other" and she walked away leaving us alone. We stood a couple of feet apart, with a Sally sized space between us. Neither of us moved. I wanted to take her hand, I actually wanted to put my arms around her and kiss her. But I would have settled for taking her hand. She looked down at the ground shyly. I started to feel slightly awkward with the silence, I should say something, anything, but what should I say, I didn't just want to blurt something stupid out again.

31

So I started rehearsing in my head something about how pretty she looked, or how I had been thinking about her all night and had agonised all day about how to see her again tonight. I probably took too long.

So she broke the silence, she also took my hand, "Come on we can go and walk Prince" she said.

I could barely hear her, I was staring into her eyes and my heart was beating in my ears like a big bass drum. She took my hand, she took MY hand. I know she said something about a walk and something about a Prince, so I just walked with her oblivious to where we were going or why. I had temporarily lost the power of speech.

Within three minutes we arrived at her sister's house on Lambhill Street. It was a ground floor house and the window was open and loud music was blasting out. There were two women with about half a dozen kids running round them standing at the window. I saw a movement out of the corner of my eye and unbelievably I saw a wolf running at us at full pace. I pulled Patricia behind me, instinctively and the wolf leapt up and pawed me on the chest and bounced off barking. It almost knocked me over. Patricia laughed behind me, a tinkle of golden bells.

"That's Prince" she said "Prince this is Danny" she added getting a hold of the dog and leaning down and petting it, rubbing it's back and putting her arms around its neck and cuddling it. Prince didn't object, why would he, I certainly wouldn't. He was a beautiful and magnificent German Shepherd dog.

We walked Prince around Kinning Park, the actual park not the district called after it. The park was a narrow strip of greenery which runs parallel to the M8 motorway which bisects Glasgow. It had a tiny swing park with three swings and a roundabout. We sat on the roundabout and talked. And talked.

"Where do you work" I asked

"In the pizza factory at Kingston" she replied

"And what do you do there" I asked.

"Make Pizza's" she replied, with a sardonic, what else? Grin. She seemed to be enjoying my discomfort, I felt like somebody who had only learned to talk moments before.

"Oh right I suppose that makes sense, you wouldn't be pickling onions I suppose" I said, my depths of witty and interesting conversation were proving very shallow when it mattered most.

"How come I haven't seen you before" I asked, staring at her, she must think I am some sort of nutcase, all I have done is stare at her, as if she is an alien from another planet or something, what was wrong with me.

"I just moved in with my sister, I come from McCulloch street, but I have sort of fell out with my Ma. Well no really fell out just got fed up with her moaning and my wee brother's an annoying wee shite, so when I got a job down here it was easier to stay down here" she said, she had no problem with normal conversation so why was I struggling so much.

"I've got three annoying wee brothers so I know what you mean about that" I said, thinking, whatever her brother is like wait till she meets Charlie then she will know what an annoying wee brother really is, in fact wait till she meets Paul and David as well. Paul was still a manky wee shite and David was turning into a right spoilt brat.

"Where's McCulloch Street?" I asked.

"In Pollokshields" she answered.

"Where's Pollokshields" I asked.

She smiled thinking I was joking, I wasn't. Darlene had moved into a flat in Pollokshields with John Lawson a year or so before, I still hadn't been there and wasn't actually sure where it was, I presumed it was somewhere near Pollok, where Donnie and Annie had moved to, maybe four years before.

"It's just up at the top of Shields road, I will show you the next time" she said.

I heard her, I definitely heard her say "the next time" I also heard how she said it, with no doubts no hesitation. There was going to be a next time. Yeeha.

We talked some more and some more and then some more again. I can't honestly recall everything we talked about. I know at one point I tried an old joke out on her.

"I am part gypsy" I smiled "On my granny's side, they were Irish gypsies before my Granny met my Granda and they settled down"

She smiled, I took her hand in one of mine and turned it face up. "Let me tell your fortune" I said.

She laughed softly, but didn't take her hand away.

"You are going to live a long life" I said, trailing my finger across her palm, tracing the lifeline as if I had a clue what I was talking about.

"You will marry young and have two children" I said, she smiled. "Your husband will be a very handsome man, quite short but very very handsome and smart" I said grinning like an idiot, she looked at me and smiled at me and with me.

"You will leave Glasgow, and live in a beautiful village in a beautiful house with a beautiful garden" I said. At this point I should have provided the punch line to the joke, and said "There will be a beautiful pond in the garden, can you see it?" at which point I should spit a little puddle into the palm of her hand. I know it isn't a very funny joke, but it got a satisfying screech out of Darlene when I played it on her. But I didn't furnish the punch line to Patricia, I just ended with the words. "And you will be very happy, with your handsome shortish husband and beautiful children in your beautiful house"

She smiled that shy smile and said "Aye right" and leapt off the roundabout to try and get a hold of Prince. I joined her in chasing after the dog, we eventually caught him and went back and sat on the swings. Just as we sat down, we saw someone approach us waving, it was Sally.

She was breathing heavily as she sat down on the third swing beside us. When she got her breath back she said "Where have you been, Betty's going mental, everybody's out looking for you"

"Why, what's happened" she asked with a puzzled and worried look on her face.

"Nothing's happened, we were all just worried about you" Sally said and added "You know that it's nearly seven o'clock in the morning, don't you, you've been out all night"

I looked at my wrist I don't know why, I didn't have a watch, but it's what you do isn't it, when someone mentions the time or asks the time you automatically look at your wrist.

"What time do you make it Danny boy, two hairs past a freckle" Sally said when she saw me look at my naked watch less wrist.

Patricia looked at me and I smiled at her, I noticed that the sky was getting lighter so Sally must be near enough telling the truth. If you had held me down and tortured me I would have sworn blind we hadn't been there more than hour or two. In fact we had been there almost nine hours. It was incredible to me and obviously also to Patricia.

"What have you two been doing all night as if I need to ask" Sally asked with a lascivious grin.
Patricia put her head down and blushed behind the curtain of her beautiful hair, and I fell in love all over again.

I saw her that night gain, I didn't bother sleeping, I couldn't. I completely forgot I had a cinema date planned with Maureen. I'm sorry Maureen, it wasn't your fault it was mine, in fact strictly speaking it wasn't even my fault it was my heart, I had no control.

I walked up to her house just as it was getting dark, it was April and the light was starting to fade at about eight o'clock and it was dark by half past. She was at the window leaning out, this was the third day in a row I had saw her and the strangest thing was that she was more beautiful each time. She saw me coming and tuned to Sally and said something she threw the cigarette she had been smoking towards the gutter and went inside. My heart dropped, I could feel a tear forming behind my eye. Then suddenly she appeared out of the close and smiled at me.

"Are you looking for me" she asked, smiling happily.

"Actually" I said, as straight faced as I could "I was wondering if I could take Prince for a walk" she eyed me with suspicion and smiled again when

I added "But you can come with us if you like, I am not sure if he will come to me when I shout"

Sally answered me "oh I think he will Danny boy, and probably not just him, either" Patricia slapped her gently on the arm and shouted in the close for Prince. He bounded out and leapt straight at Patricia paws in the air, tail wagging and slobbering with excitement. The only difference between us was that I didn't have a tail.

We visited the park again. Our quiet place, and it was quiet, it was dark. We didn't stay as long we were both working the next day. We didn't talk as much, we couldn't. We were kissing too much. I floated all the way home after leaving her at her sisters. I may have stood outside her window talking to her all night if her brother in law Tommy hadn't told her to shut the window and get in she had work in the morning. She went in and closed the window, five minutes later Tommy opened it again and said "Are you going to stand their all night son, or are you going home, you have got work in the morning as well, I suppose"

I grinned a moron's grin at him and walked away, I bumped into Charlie and Iris on my way home. Charlie was walking Iris to the Gorbals where she lived, it was after ten o'clock. I offered to walk to the Gorbals with them, it wasn't the safest place in the world to be when it was dark even for Charlie. But he pointed out to me quite forcibly that he had managed alright for the last year and a half, so he was sure he would manage tonight. He asked me a few times if I was drunk, I had a weird look on my face and my eyes looked funny. I didn't have the words to tell him then, that I was drunk on love, intoxicated by desire.

I tried my best to avoid Maureen all morning but as it was my week in the finishing hall I couldn't, and she eventually stood in front of me with a tray of finished products for me to inspect.

"I'm sorry" I said sheepishly "I was playing football yesterday and we went for a few pints after it, and I ended up a wee bit drunk and fell asleep in the chair, and never woke up until half past ten" As excuses went I thought it was good, it had enough detail to be true, but it was still quite simple, I was reasonably pleased with it and thought it would work.

"Is that right" she said "And what position does Patricia Miller play in this team" I was stunned, how the hell could she know that? That's just not possible. Maureen lived in Cardonald, what was going on here. She gave me a look of disgust and the girl behind her dumped her tray on my desk and walked away just as disgusted. I looked at the tag and it said Shirley McFadyen. The name rang a bell. Of course McFadyen was Sally's name, this lassie must be related to her. What were the chances of that, I was gobsmacked.

Shirley McFadyen brushed past me when I was stood in the queue in the canteen.

"Lying two timing rat" she said jabbing the corner of her brown wooden tray into my back.

"How can I two time somebody I haven't even went out with yet" I shouted at her, clearly letting my guilt get the better of me. I wasn't guilty about two timing her but I had made up a lie as to why I hadn't appeared and left her standing at Boots on her own. I really did feel terrible about that as I should I suppose. My outburst had caused most people in the canteen to look at me, and it was almost entirely women, I could feel the disapproval coming off them in waves. I got my cup of tea and a wee three pack of Bourbon Cream biscuits and went and sat down. I chose a table with three older women, to avoid the wrath and disgust of the girls my age, I could see it in their faces, and it was like I did a walk of shame the length of the canteen.

Every time I slowed down and even looked like going to sit down, I got a glare. Oran empty chair was suddenly pulled under the table making it clear I wasn't welcome. When I did sit down beside the three older women, they were smiling at me, well laughing really, but not letting it out.

"Who's been a naughty Danny boy the" witch number one said with a wee cackle.

I lifted my tray and said "And you'se three can fuck off as well then" I went to stand up and leave in a nice dramatic huff, but witch number two put her hand on my arm and made me sit down again. Witch number three said "Forget it son, it will blow over by tomorrow, your young two timing isnae a big thing when you're young"

"I wisnae fucking two timing" I said and regretted swearing immediately these women were ages with my Ma. "I'm sorry for swearing, but I wisnae two timing, I arranged to meet Maureen to go to the pictures last night, but I met a lassie on Friday and spent the weekend with her, and just forgot about Maureen, but that's no two timing, I hidnae even been out with Maureen yet, that canny be two timing can it" I asked them, feeling as if my reputation was on the line.

Witch number two said "Spent the weekend with this lassie did you" and licked her lips like a big water buffalo or something she never had a tooth in her head so her tongue looked huge and grotty as she licked her big fat lips. I avoided telling her how disgusting that was but still went beetroot red and stammered "Not like that, not like spent the weekend as in actually spent the whole weekend, I mean I seen her every night, but not seen her like seen her, I talked to her every night that's all"

"What no kissing at all, in three nights you're a bit slow off the mark are you no" witch number three said, and I went redder.

"I remember just after the war" witch number one said "When I had a few American soldiers after me"

Witch number two cackled and licked her lips again "A few, the way I heard it you had more American soldiers than Eisenhower" All three of them went into a combined cackle which could quite possibly wake witches all over Europe up.

"Aye you might be right Patricia, I did have quite a few in the end up" Witch number one said, "but what I was going to say was"

I interrupted her "Is your name Patricia" I asked witch number two, looking at her gumsy mouth her wire brush hair and the hairs on her chin.

"Aye" she said, and the penny dropped "Is that your wee lassies name then" and all three of them cackled again. If I was a decent engineer I could harness the energy in those cackles and power all the machines in the factory. When they stopped Witch number one wiped the tears from her eyes and said "Gonny let me finish, I was trying to say that when I was dating Americans, because that's what they called it dating, the first two nights were a wee kiss, but the third night he usually got a wee squeeze of my boobies" as she said this she grabbed my hand and rubbed it on her chest. I almost wet my pants and I screamed like a banshee and pulled away from her.

This sent the three of them into supersonic cackling, I was surprised there wasn't green smoke coming out of their ears. I looked at the hand she had rubbed on her chest as if it would show scorch marks or scars of embarrassment. I indicated my disgust at them with a disdainful look that not one of them noticed and I skulked out of the canteen. For months afterwards I would get asked if I enjoyed feeling big Aggie's boobs and did I still fantasise about jiggling them about, and that was just from the women. They were disgusting creatures all of them. Ugh.

I didn't see Patricia again until Thursday and even then it was only for ten minutes. I had ironically fallen asleep in the living room armchair on Monday night so didn't see her then. Worked late Tuesday night so didn't see her then , she worked late Wednesday night so I didn't see her then. I was a bit paranoid walking down to her house on the Thursday, thinking she was avoiding me, even though on the Monday and Tuesday it was me that was at fault sort of.

As I approached her house I saw one of her nieces shoot into the close shouting "Patricia's boyfriend is here, Patricia's boyfriend is here." That cheered me up. A lot.

The window went up and she popped her head and shoulders out, her bare head and shoulders. She had a towel wrapped round her neck like a turban and another wrapped round her body like a sarong, even though I didn't know what a sarong was then. I stared at her, just for a change. I stared at the sweep of her beautiful neck, in clear view without her hair hiding its elegance and length, I stared at her beautiful shoulders and at the point where her towel crossed her chest, hiding untold delights. I gulped. I think that was the point when I decided that I had met the most beautiful girl in the world and that opinion has never changed, ever.

"What are you staring at" she asked, looking down at her chest and flicking a bit of lint from the towel off of it. I wanted to say the poetry that

I felt inside. I wanted to say, you, I am looking at you. I am looking at all of you and seeing my future, my life my all. But since she was surrounded by a bunch of staring nieces and nephews with inquisitive eyes and ears, I said "Nothing, I'm not staring at anything"

"Right then" she said, unconvinced. "I am just out of the bath, I need to go down to my Granny's later to see my Ma. Do you want to do something tomorrow night?"

I nodded enthusiastically, this was starting to get embarrassing. "Aye, that's what I came down for, do you want to come to a party tomorrow night" I said abruptly.

I heard her brother in law shouting in the background "Who's at that fucking window, it's freezing in here" I heard one of his daughters reply to him "its Patricia's boyfriend"

This brought a smile to my lips which transferred to Patricia's lips, "Am I, your boyfriend" I asked her.

"I don't know" she said softly "That's up to you isn't it"

"Well if it's up to me then yes I am and you need to come to the party now." I said with a grin on my face that might stay there for a while if not forever.

"Ok" was all she said and turned away from the window but glanced back with a smile before her brother and law scowled at me and slammed the window closed.

"What party" I asked myself as I walked home. My Da had gone back up to Sullom Voe on Monday with Donnie and Dunky. My ma was heading down to Redcar on Friday on the two o'clock train, to spend a week with Dorothy, she was taking wee David with her but leaving Paul with me and Charlie. Paul was twelve now so he was no bother, he wasn't mental the way Charlie was when he was twelve. The worst you could expect from Paul was that he would stick his finger so far up his nose looking for snotters that he might actually pick a wee bit of his brains out. Or that he would break something practicing his jiving. He thought he was a reincarnation of Elvis. Uh Huh.

40

I picked her up from her sisters at about half eight and we went to the Fountain bar for a drink. I found out she was only sixteen, she looked twenty one. Not that it mattered I had been drinking in the Fountain since I was sixteen. I had been drinking in the Jester along at Ibrox since I was fifteen, in fact I used to hide my schoolbag in a hedge in the street next to the Jester at lunch time and go in for a pint and pie "n" peas.

Most of my pals from Cessnock were in the Fountain that night, and I couldn't have felt more proud. Patricia looked absolutely gorgeous. I was in a bit of a daze most of the night moving from table to table with Patricia introducing her and basically letting everybody know she was with me and was my girlfriend. A slightly awkward moment when Gordon Differ sniggered and said he hoped I had plenty of money with me, that was quickly resolved when I tipped the pint in front of him over his trousers and told him to go home and get changed because he looked like he had pished himself.

We left just before the pub closed and walked along the Paisley road, it took us a while because I made up a rule that we weren't allowed to walk past a lamp post without stopping at it and having a kiss. When I realised that there was about fifty yards between lamp posts, I added phone boxes electricity boxes and traffic lights to the rules. We eventually got home to the empty house, Paul had told me before I went out that he was staying with one of his pals in Middleton Street.

"Where's the party" Patricia asked, when I turned the light on in the living room.

"Here" I answered, spreading my arms and indicating the living room.

"Who's coming" she asked.
"Us" I said.

I smiled and sat down on the couch, she looked slightly perturbed but sat down beside me, and the kissing resumed. Obviously being eighteen I had no control over my wandering hands. But Patricia had an iron grip and exercised complete control over them, she made it very clear that kissing was as far as it went. She let me know she had never gone further than kissing and had no intention in doing so anytime soon. I didn't care kissing was plenty for me, just being in the same room was plenty, kissing was a bonus.

We spent just about every available minute for the next four or five months together. She met my Ma, and Darlene and we found out that her and Darlene already knew each other. Patricia had even done some babysitting for Darlene, because Patricia's mum lived on the same street in Pollokshields as Darlene did.

Darlene seemed a bit jealous because Patricia was much better looking than her, it didn't help I suppose that Darlene was heavily pregnant with her second child and probably felt as bloated as she looked. They had quite a bit in common with each other, including the habit of saying slightly the wrong thing, so I was sure they would get on okay. I couldn't really read my Ma's thoughts about Patricia at first, she seemed okay with her but time would tell.

It turned out Charlie also knew Patricia fairly well, apparently he had spent some time in Pollokshields because he had pals who lived there, which was news to me, but most things that Charlie did now were news to me. Patricia and Iris, Charlie's girlfriend, seemed wary of each other but overall they seemed to be relatively okay as well. Paul liked her straight away because she gave him a packet of chewing gum, which helped with his Elvis impersonations. Wee David also liked her but that was because she gave him a cuddle and his head was in her boobs, so he was as much in love with her as I was. He was only ten but already had a stash of dirty books under his bed. To be fair I think they used to be mine.

By amazing coincidence it turned out that Patricia's sister and brother in law, Betty and Tommy, were virtually best pals, with my eldest brother Donnie and his wife Annie. I found this out one Friday night when I was in Betty and Tommy's house waiting for Patricia to finish getting ready we were going to the pictures. I was sitting on the edge of a double bed which was in an alcove off the family living room, Betty and Tommy had five kids aged from one to about ten so the living room wasn't the tidiest room I had ever seen, it was clean but there were toys or clothes from the kids everywhere.

Which explains why I was sat on the edge of the bed, it was the only place in the room that had a clear space to sit. Patricia's best pal Sally came in with another three of their pals, it was Friday night and they had started drinking early and were on their way into town.

"Hey Dan" Sally said sitting beside me and putting her arm around my shoulder. She was the only person ever to call me Dan, I didn't like it and she knew it, my mistake was letting her know I didn't like it.

"Do you want to just piss off to the Fountain with your pig ignorant smelly arsed mates and let Patricia come out with us" she asked sweetly, whilst giving me a kiss on the cheek.

"Naw" I said just as sweetly.

"How no" she asked petulantly but still smiling sweetly.

"Because you are a bunch of drunken tramps and she is a sweet innocent child, you'se will corrupt her" I said "If I let her go into the town with you'se, she will be on the game within a week" I added, laughing.

Sally decided the best way to get me to change my mind was to start tickling me.

"Oh go on Dan, let her come with us, you know you want to, we can teach her how to make you happy" Sally said as she started tickling me under my arms and then in my belly, as I turned away from her to avoid her probing fingers, one of her pals joined in, so I was stuck between the two of them, I edged further on to the bed and was wriggling like mad to try and stop both of them from tickling me, the next thing I know is that Patricia has arrived in the living room and decided to join in along with the other two girls who had been watching with hilarity. So now I am squirming like mad with five girls trying to tickle me, I am laughing so much that I am pretty sure I have thirty seconds to escape before I literally pish my pants.

And that's when Donnie walked in, and that's the circumstances under which he met Patricia. I think that image of me in bed with five teenage girls all tickling me sustained his fantasies for years afterwards. The matter was resolved when Sally asked Patricia if she wanted to go out with her and the rest of their pals or go to the boring pictures with me.

"What's it to be Patty, the boring pictures with boring Dan, or out on the razz with your best pals and her backing singers" Sally said throwing her arms round two of the backing singers.

"I'm not going out with you'se lot" Patricia said.

"How no" Sally asked, disappointed.

"Cause you'se are a bunch of tramps and would have me on the game within a week" she said and both of us left, laughing.

I popped my head in the window as we passed and said "Donnie, that bed's empty now, see how many lassies you can get in it" Patricia slapped the back of my head, and Sally screeched with laughter "We don't do geriatrics, unless it's a bed bath he wants" she howled with more of her high pitched laughter, Donnie didn't look too chuffed.

When we left the house I did ask Patricia that if she wanted to go out with her pals, I was fine with it. I would just go for a few pints with Donnie and see her the next day, she said no, she had been looking forward to the pictures with me all week and that was that, she did look back when we turned out of Lambhill street, just as Sally and the other three emerged from the close singing 'I will survive' at the very top of their very terrible voices, she had a tiny look of regret in her eyes but it was gone in a flash and didn't last until the next corner, she took my arm and we walked into town.

That turned out to be an exceptionally good night for me because not only did Patricia choose a night at the pictures with me over a night on the lash with her pals, we also found an all-night horror movie night was on at the Classic Grand cinema in Jamaica Street. It was just by chance that we walked along Jamaica street and seen it advertised, because it wasn't a cinema either of us had used before, in fact it was one most people avoided as it was best known for blue movies.

The all night horror movies didn't even start until half ten so we spent the night wandering around the city centre with a bag of chips and a can of coke. If there's a better way to spend an evening than walking around Glasgow with a bag of chips a can of coke and the most beautiful girl in the world then I haven't found it yet.

The all night horror movies were mainly rubbish, old Hammer Horror movies or low budget dubbed movies, with Carrie and The Exorcist being the exceptions. The Exorcist, a story of a young teenage girl possessed by a demon, particularly terrified Patricia, there was a scene where the girl completely swivelled her head around three hundred and sixty degrees, which was accompanied by a creaking sound apparently made by her bones being bent out of shape I assume. Patricia snuggled up very close to me during that scene, very close indeed.

So it was probably that reaction that she had that made me think it would be funny during the walk home to re-enact that scene complete with sound effects.

"Did you hear that" I said as we walked along Scotland Street towards Pollokshields, we were going to her Ma's house, because Patricia wanted to fetch more clothes to take to her sister's house where she was now staying almost full time. Particularly more knickers, she told me, because there were about five women in her sister's house and they all just helped themselves to whatever underwear came out of the washing machine. Patricia being particularly fastidious would never wear underwear that someone else had worn, so frequently ran out of acceptable underwear.

"Hear what?" she asked, timidly looking around us.

Scotland Street at that time was quite a dark and dismal place at five o'clock in the morning, it was mostly filled with factories, and an old Victorian school.

"That noise" I said, "a creaking noise"

Patricia grasped my arm and moved much closer, looking all around and especially at her feet, I later learned that she has a pathological fear of rats, so that's why she was continually looking down and flinching at every shadow.

So when she heard me making a creaking sound and looked up to find me slowly swivelling my head like the girl in the film, she freaked out. She pushed me away from her and ran about twenty yards away screaming. When I started laughing she calmed down quite quickly and came back towards me slowly, waiting no doubt for me to do something else equally stupid.

But this presented me with a major dilemma because as she had run away the buttons on her blouse had opened from top to bottom almost. Exposing her bra and much more flesh than she had dared to expose to me so far. I was overjoyed at the revealing of my version of heaven on earth, not only was Patricia the most beautiful girl in the world, it was a very happy coincidence that she also had the most beautiful body in the world and I was getting the most glorious view imaginable.

That what's caused my dilemma, should I be a gentleman and tell her about her blouse, or should I let her snuggle up to me again and perhaps enjoy the view all the way up Scotland Street and Shields road. I was so engrossed in my private fantasy world that I forgot to mention it for at least fifteen minutes and eventually only did so, because there were a few cars and trucks appearing on the road and there's no way they were enjoying the same view as me. I managed to convince her that the buttons had popped only seconds before and that I had looked away instantly to save her modesty.

Once the blushes had left her face and we settled back into an arm in arm walking pace, she told me why The Exorcist had frightened her so much. It was because the house we were going to, her mother's attic flat at one hundred and fifteen McCulloch Street, was haunted. I dismissed her assertion that the house was haunted in a typically robust fashion.

"Don't tell me you believe in ghosts and spirits and all that shite" I said laughing.

She looked up at me calmly with a knowing smile and said "Wait and see"


## Chapter 19.  115 McCulloch Street, the haunted house.

That morning we were in and out of her Ma's house in less than half an hour all that we were there for was so that Patricia could grab some clothes so we didn't hang about for long. I said a quick hello to her Ma, who was up that early because she was on her way to a cleaning job. I never met Patricia's brother who was about thirteen, it was six in the morning he was still asleep.

I had a brief glance around her Ma's place, it was an attic flat, accessed through a normal front door on the third floor of the tenements in McCulloch Street. But once inside that front door there was a steep and narrow flight of stairs which had thirteen steps, I only noticed that later when it seemed significant. When you reached the top of those stairs on your immediate left was the bathroom, a small and cramped space, immaculately clean. On your right was the living room door, once in the living room there was another door accessing a short hallway leading to two bedrooms.

During this first glance the first feature I noticed and the most striking was the sloping ceilings, all of the rooms had severely sloping ceilings which seemed to make them much smaller, because the further away you got from the centre of the room and the nearer you got to the walls the lower the ceiling became. Meaning that you couldn't actually stand upright in certain corners of the room, the second thing I noticed was how dull it was. Although it was early morning this was a fine May morning and the sun was shining outside, but not much of that sunlight reached the centre of the rooms thanks to the dormer style windows. The third thing I noticed was that it was freezing, I mean really freezing, it's the only house I have ever been in where I put a coat on when I came in rather than taking a coat off, and it was like that whether it was July or January.

I was only in there for half an hour but I shivered as we left. I didn't say to Patricia that I found it quite creepy, that would have been too cheeky even for me. I didn't come back to the house for about another four weeks but Patricia and her sister filled me in on some of the previous ghostly goings on later on that night.

"The worst one I can remember is when I woke up in the middle of the night, feeling really scared. I must have been about six or seven. I shared a bedroom with Rob, my wee brother he would have been about three I think. Anyway I woke up and sat straight up, I don't know if I heard something that woke me up or if I t was just something in my head telling me to wake up. I got up and ran the few steps to my Ma's door, but when I got outside my Ma's door I just stopped and listened." Patricia was staring into the middle distance as she was telling me this, as if it was playing out on a screen behind her eyes, she cradled a cup of tea and had a cigarette between her fingers as she talked.

"I didn't know for sure what the noise was, I want to say it sounded like my Ma sobbing, but I think that's what I am telling myself now. At the time the next morning I told my Ma I heard a wee lassie crying and that the wee lassie sounded just like me" She took a long pull on her cigarette, and I was so close to her I could almost see the six year old Patricia in her eyes, I know she was seeing her behind them.

She hesitated, gathering her thoughts or maybe her memories. "I stood with my hand on the doorknob, listening, I didn't want to go in, but I knew that I had to, I was scared really scared, but I was torn between running back to my bed and burying myself under the blankets on my bed or making a run for my Ma's bed. What made up my mind was Rob sitting up in bed and starting to cry. He wasn't wailing or anything, like he does sometimes. He just sat up and started wiping his eyes with the sleeve of his pyjamas; he was like just sobbing to himself. I nearly ran over to him but I heard another sound from behind my Ma's bedroom door, like a wee cry of pain, like something you would do if you banged your toe or something, it wisnae a loud scream or anything, just a wee sort of yelp" She took another sip of tea and another long draw on her cigarette.

My knee was pressed against her leg and I felt the slightest of shivers run down her, I was completely enthralled, I didn't want to do anything that would bring her out of where she was. Where she had put herself to bring back a total recall of what happened, she spoke as if it had all happened that morning rather than ten years before. I wanted to put my arm around her shoulder or her waist and pull her a bit closer reassure her that this was long gone, and that nothing could happen to her while I was there. But I couldn't take the chance of breaking the spell. There was a look of fear in her eyes, not terror just fear. It appeared to me that picking at the memories was frightening her as much as the memories themselves.

"I pushed the door open firmly, believing that whatever was there would be frightened by the door banging against the wall and that they wouldn't know it was a little girl behind the door. I remember actually thinking that, thinking I need to make them believe I'm a big girl, and I am a big girl, because I am six now and six is the age of a big girl. It had been my birthday just days before this, and everybody had been saying that's you

48

six now sweetheart, you're a big girl now" Another sip of tea and another drag on her cigarette, she gathered herself for the end.

"My Ma was sat up against her head board, almost sideways against the headboard, her eyes were closed, and just as I banged the door open I saw her blankets slide gently off the bottom of her bed and drop to the floor. I never thought about this until years later, when I helped my Ma make her bed one morning. My Ma had two big thick blankets on her bed, they could have been army blankets if they weren't pale pink with a sort of satin band across the top. When my Ma made her bed she had a bottom sheet and then a top sheet and then the two blankets, well two in the winter and one in the summer. But that night there was two, because my birthday is November so she would have had two. The point is when my Ma made her bed she tucked the sheets and blankets right under the mattress. I can remember sometimes climbing in beside my Ma in the middle of the night and struggling to get under the blanket because she tucked it under the mattress so tight.

"So when I saw the blankets slide off the bottom of the bed, that shouldn't have been able to happen, you would need a tractor or a few big guys to pull they blankets off that bed from the bottom of the bed, they couldn'y slide off like that they just couldn'y. I looked away from the blankets back towards my Ma, she was sort of waving her arms in front of her, her side was pressed up against the headboard and she was, I don't know how to describe it, it was like she was shooing something away with her hands. Her arms were straight out and her hands were palm down and she was like just flicking her wrists and fingers as if your dog was sniffing at your feet or something and you were trying to make it go away, it was like that, but her eyes were still shut" Patricia paused again trying to gather her thoughts.

"I know it must have been a dream, because what my Ma done next could only be in a dream"

"Did she fart?"

This came from Tommy, Patricia's brother in law, and he was absolutely delighted with his joke, he was rocking back and forward on the edge of his seat laughing his head off. I grimly smiled to myself, he had probably heard this tale repeated a hundred times and wasn't as caught up in it as I was, his joke had drained the tension from the moment and from me. I looked back at Patricia and she had a tear in the corner of her eye.

"Finish what you were saying hen" Betty, her sister told her "Tell Danny what happened next, he was on tender hooks there, I was watching his eyes getting bigger and bigger I thought they were gonny pop out" and she was just as pleased with her contribution as her husband was with his. Patricia looked a bit crestfallen. She had been in the moment, she hadn't been in Betty's living room with us she had been in her Ma's bedroom. Revisiting her nightmare if that's what it was, maybe hoping to make some sense of it. I had been right beside her as well.

I put my arm around her waist and pulled her closer if that was possible, my leg seemed welded to hers. "Tell me what happened" I said softly kissing her on the lips. Somebody sniggered.

"No, it was only a dream I'll tell you some other time, their all making a fool of me now, come on we'll take Prince out for a walk" she said and stood up abruptly almost causing me to fall off the couch. I was a bit angry if I'm honest, I felt deflated, I was right there with her reliving every breath and every creak and seeing every pale shadow. Tommy and Betty had spoiled that with their flippancy and upset Patricia into the bargain, I wasn't very happy, they had no right to upset her like that.

We took the dog out even though it was pouring down, we rushed from shop doorway to shop doorway along Paisley Road, urging Prince to do his business, so we could return to the relative comfort of the house. As we huddled in a doorway and Patricia shouted at the dog "Gonny just pee, you mongrel, it's freezing out here" Prince just came in beside us sat on his haunches and licked her hand which was folded in mine trying to grab some warmth.

"I don't think I would want to pee against a steel lamppost in all this rain either" I said smiling at her, "Come on we will just head back, he will do it when he needs it enough. Unless you want to tell me the rest of your story, I can give you a wee cuddle and get you heated up a bit first if you like" I held her chin up to look in her eyes. She looked into my eyes and couldn't fail to see the hunger and desire, and she surprised me, by not pushing me away as was her usual response to my lascivious advances.

"Later" she said, and kissed me, long and deep. This upset prince so much that he raised his leg and peed all over the shop door we were leaning against. "Your dog's a jealous monster" I said. She kissed me again just a peck on the lips smiled her secret smile, the one that was just for me and said "So am I, be careful"

We hurriedly took Prince back home to Tommy and Betty's, he thanked us for taking him out by shaking all the rain out of his coat as he stood in front of us while we sat on the couch trying to get warm. We were alone in the living room well virtually alone, her two young nieces were watching "Are you being served" on the telly. I was young enough to think they weren't hanging on our every word

"Do you want to come and stay at mine tonight" She looked at me closely, she knew what I was asking, she gave it some thought. We had been going out for almost six months now and had progressed slightly from kissing but only slightly. She nodded her head and gave me a nervous and shy smile. I squeezed her hand and smiled back.

Despite the rain, we took our time wandering along Govan road towards my house, and we talked. Probably for the very first time, we properly talked. Up to then it had been banter and kisses, gentle probing, but that night we talked. The talking continued when we got to my house and lay on top of my bed.

"Do you like me" she asked timidly, she was facing me. I had both arms around her holding her close her head was on my shoulder. Before I could answer she asked again, "Do you like me enough that you won't dump me tomorrow because you have had what you want."

I felt a surge of emotion, it was a combination of hurt and guilt, how could she think that, how could she not know how I felt about her. How was that even possible, I had only known her six months or so and already every single thing in my life was organised around her. Every minute I was working I thought about how long it would be until I saw her. Every minute I wasn't working I tried to spend with her, how could she think I didn't like her enough.

I was eighteen it was a lesson I still struggled for many years to learn, she didn't know because I never told her. I was so wrapped up with loving her that I never took time to tell her. I then saw that as a fault of hers because she should know that I love her, by my actions by my deeds, she shouldn't need to be told, I made it obvious enough. I was wrong, for a very long time I was wrong, she did need to be told everybody needs to be told, sometimes, just sometimes words speak louder than actions.

I squeezed her just a little bit tighter and whispered into her hair "Of course I like you, can't you tell. I like you more than anybody I have ever met, or anybody I have ever seen, ever. "

I was too young to get everything she was telling me, but I felt her vulnerability intensely. "I will always like you Patricia, no matter whatever happens in our lives, and I will never dump you, you might have to shoot me if you ever want rid of me."

"Do you love me" she asked with such depth of longing that even at my tender age I could hear the question underneath her question. Her body stiffened slightly as she waited for me to answer. She desperately needed to be loved and I was more than happy to do that.

"Yes I do, more than anything I honestly do" I whispered into her ear and held her even tighter.

"Then we should do it" she said, kissed me and snuggled closer.

"We will" I said "Just not tonight, I want you tell me the end of your ghost story and then I want a cuddle and a sleep, I'm just about knocked out after being up all last night at the pictures" I kissed the top of her head and she told me the end of her tale.

"Where did I get to" she asked.

"Your Ma was pressed up against the headboard trying to shoo something away, from the way you explained it. There was something at the side of her bed that she could see and you couldn'y but her eyes were shut so she must have been dreaming" I said encouraging her.

"No, it was a bit like that, I could see that her eyes were shut, but I don't think she was sleeping. I think she didnae want to open her eyes. But she did, she opened her eyes and stood up on the bed, I mean just stood straight up. I was only six and it was dark and I was scared, but it looked to me as if she stood up without using her hands. Her hands were still out in front of her, but she had been pressed against the headboard. How could she possibly just stand straight up? I screamed" Patricia whispered the last two words and fell silent.

I waited what seemed to be a few minutes but was probably only ten seconds. "Are you asleep" I whispered.

"No" she answered, "I screamed, Ma, ma, ma, something like that, and my Ma's eyes opened. She whipped her head to the left as if she was watching something in the corner of the room and then she whipped it to her right as if it had sped past me and out of the bedroom door. I was terrified, I tried to scream but nothing came out, I must have looked as if I was in a silent movie, my mouth and eyes were wide open but there was no sound. And then we heard a big crashing noise, it was coming from my bedroom, the room where Rob was." Patricia again hesitated and her breath hitched a little. I held her.

"It was a big old fashioned chest of drawers, a tallboy it's called, that had fell over, not completely because the drawers had all come out of it and it stood at an angle, if the drawers had been closed it would have been face down on the floor. Rob was three or maybe nearly four, it's possible that he had been climbing on it and it toppled. But since he was sitting up in his bed just pointing at it, I don't think that's what happened." She said holding on to my hand and tucking it under her chin in both of hers.

"So what do you think happened then" I asked gently.

"I don't know Danny, I just don't know" she said "Maybe I dreamed it all"

"But what happened after it, what did your Ma tell people about it? Did you tell her everything?" I asked. "Did you tell her about wakening up and feeling something was wrong, did you tell her about her standing straight up?"

"Not really, not until years after it" she answered. "The very next day, two of my Aunties came up, My Aunt Doris, she's lovely you will like her and my Aunt Sarah, she's like a second Ma to me. My Ma sat and had a cup of tea with them, and I was sat behind the couch playing with my wee dolly and I heard what she told them." Patricia paused apparently gathering her thoughts.

"She told them that I had climbed up on the chest of drawers and toppled it over and that I had frightened the life out of her and Rob, she didnae know what I was up to it was three in the morning and she was starting work at half six. I couldn't understand why she was saying that, I was in her room when the tallboy fell, she pushed past me to get into the other room. I asked her why she had said that when I was about twelve or something. She told me I was havering that she woke up when she heard the crash and when she came into the room, I was standing beside Rob's bed looking guilty, but that wisnae true Danny it wisnae" She almost sobbed.

"I know it isnae baby, I believe you" I said. We fell asleep.

The next morning was a very important one in my life not only did we consummate our relationship, we decided to get engaged. We were sitting in the kitchen in an armchair beside the fire it was a cold Sunday morning, my Ma was frying up some bacon and eggs for my Da. I had promised Patricia some French toast as soon as my Ma was finished at the cooker. Charlie came bouncing into the kitchen.

"Me and Iris are getting married" he said, opening the fridge and lifting out a two pint carton of milk which he almost demolished in one swallow.

"Don't drink all that milk, I'm gonny make French toast" I said, more concerned at a lack of milk than his news. He looked at me and grinned getting the message.

"Good thinking Danny boy, bring some ben for me and Iris, she's starving now that she's eating for two" he said and giggled as he dropped his bombshell and left the kitchen. Patricia gasped, I looked at my Ma, who didn't seem very shocked.

She looked back at me and gave a tight smile "Darlene suspected as much" she said.

"Well she should know since she's just had her second wean in two years" I said. Darlene had just given birth to Charlene a few weeks before. I don't know how Darlene had seen Iris though. I hadn't seen Darlene since she had the wean, in fact I hadn't even seen the wean yet. Annie had announced the week before that she was pregnant again and due at Christmas or thereabouts, that would be five her and Donnie had, for such a wee guy, everything was working alright.

"What age is Iris?" Patricia whispered her question in my ear.

"Eighteen" my Ma answered "There's no point in whispering if you are going to be in this family hen, it's hard enough to be bloody heard when you scream"

Patricia blushed and looked at me "Am I going to be in this family" she asked with a mischievous grin.

"Of course you are" I said exuberantly "Why don't we have a double wedding with Charlie, that would be a right laugh"

"Okay then" she whispered and looked worriedly at my Ma, I don't know why she thought it had anything to do with my Ma. It wisnae her that was asking her to get married, it was me.

It was the end of November, we decided with Charlie and Iris that we would get married in July, none of us thought about the fact that Iris would be either heavily pregnant by then or just getting over having her wean. Charlie had been a bit quick in announcing her pregnancy she was only about two weeks late, but they both said they knew. They claimed to have been trying for a few months.

We decided to have a joint engagement party as well, at Hogmanay in my Ma's house, it was Charlie's idea. An engagement party was a must because people get you engagement presents and if you invite enough people and get enough presents they can be sold and that helps to pay for the wedding. I hadn't thought of that bit, paying for a wedding. I was still an apprentice, I wasn't making much. Patricia had jacked in the job in the pizza factory and got a job in the bingo hall, she preferred the bingo hall because it wasn't as smelly as the pizza factory but the money wasn't great.

So how could we afford to get married, was the main question, there were other things we hadn't thought about as well. Like where would we live, what would we live on because both of us had low wages. If we did get a council house how would we furnish it? We had the same answer for all of those questions which was, that something would turn up it can't be that hard everybody else manages.

Dunky advised me to get her checked for madness after what happened to his missus. Donnie told me to make sure she knew who was boss and don't let her start making the rules or my life would be a misery. My Ma told me I was being ridiculous, I was far too young, I had a career to try and build before I even thought about getting married. She refused to believe that Patricia wasn't pregnant, everybody did. Dorothy even phoned me from Redcar and told me that I didn't have to get married just because she was pregnant, that was old fashioned. And why were we hiding it, it would only be a matter of time before it was noticeable.

My ma crossed the line one night when she told me Patricia was too interested in herself to make a good wife. When I shouted at my Ma that she didn't even know her and that she had no right to talk about her. My Ma explained that if we had weans, then Patricia would probably be expecting me to look after them, while she did her hair and makeup, because that's all she was interested in. I shouted at my Ma that she was wrong and if she didn't like Patricia then she shouldn't bother coming to the wedding.

That wee spat lasted for two weeks, before I apologised to my Ma for shouting at her but assured her that she was wrong about Patricia. Unfortunately Patricia undermined my argument that night by taking two and a half hours to get ready, until I was actually shouting at her that her hair was lovely and she needed to move before the pub was shut. My Ma shook her head at me as we eventually went out. I just smiled sheepishly and slapped Patricia on the bum as we left. That was another great reason to get married that I couldn't really explain very well to my Ma. Patricia's bum.

We had to go round a few of Patricia's family so that they could meet me, this was also Charlie's idea. If they met me they would feel obliged to get us a present even if they didn't come to the engagement party. It turned out he was right about that, very few came to the party but most of them handed some sort of present into her ma's house.

What did happen when we went round these aunties and uncles was that they were all keen to tell me their ghost stories about the attic flat at 115 McCulloch Street. Even Betty, Patricia's sister told us a wee tale one night, despite her trying to make a fool of Patricia the last time we talked about it.

"It was what happened to my Abigail that frightened the shite out of me, I never went back up to her house for ages after that." Betty said, stopped to light a fag and brush all the ash from her last one off her knee. "I was staying the night, we had a wee problem with the electric, it wisnae really a wee problem, it was a big problem because it was cut off" she paused to have a good laugh at her joke.

"Anyway we were staying the night and we all had to sleep in the living room, well me and the two lassie had to sleep in the living room, Tommy just stayed in our own house without the electric but he was steaming so he didnae care at all" she paused again to drink some of her tea and puff on her fag.

Right so we had to sleep on the floor in the living room, my ma put down a spare mattress she had and the three of us slept on that. The lassies were sleeping well early probably just after nine, I sat up and had a fag and a gab with my Ma like you do" she said giggling. "So it was probably after midnight before I fell asleep." I woke up at three o'clock on the dot, I know it was three o'clock because I had left the light on the electric fire on, so it wisnae too dark for the weans" She paused.

"Too dark for the weans that had fallen asleep at nine o'clock or do you mean too dark for you" I asked chuckling.

She chuckled back "Aye maybe it was too dark for me, hee hee. Well anyway it was exactly three o'clock and I stretched out to cuddle the lassies, and I could only find Margaret I couldn't find Abigail, and I got feart. I shouted her name, I thought maybe she had wandered off the mattress and on to the couch, she was only three but, so I got a bit panicky. I ran into my ma's room and couldn't see her and I ran into Patricia and Rob's room and I couldn't see her. So by now I was freaking out. The only place left was the hall or the toilet but she couldn't be out there because I had jammed a chair under the living room door handle." She looked a bit agitated now, and lit another fag using the one she was just finishing to light it.

"I looked round at the living room door and it was open, that scared me for two reasons, obviously because I had jammed the chair in it, but mostly because the reason I jammed the chair in it was to keep the weans in here away from the stairs down to the front door, They are way too steep and really dangerous for the weans. I just about flew across that room and ripped the living room door open, I looked down at the bottom of the stairs expecting to see Abigail crumpled in a broken heap at the bottom. I couldn't see all the way to the bottom, it was too dark. I tried the hall light but it wisnae working, there was a wee bit of light coming from the living room but not much." Betty actually looked scared now, even though this incident had taken place about eight years before she looked really scared.

"The toilet door was lying open a wee bit but the light was off in there, but I thought if I put the light on in the toilet then it would shine down to the bottom of the stairs. So I did, and then I let out a scream" As she said this she grabbed my arm and dug her fingers in, she had me scared now.

"Abigail was sitting on the toilet with her knickers round her ankles, having a pee. She was playing with a wee cheap necklace, it was metal but not gold or silver or anything. I didn't notice it at first, I just grabbed Abi and pulled her up to my chest and kept kissing her. I carried her into the living room and sat down in the chair with her, the chair that had been jammed under the door handle and was now back under the dinner table where it was before I moved it" She released my arm from her grip which was a relief.

"So I sat her on my knee and said to her, Abi baby how did you move that chair and get out to the toilet" Betty looked straight at me and said "Do you know what she said?" I shook my head. "She said 'The lady did it, the lady came to the bed and woke me up, and then moved the chair and took me to the toilet, and she gave me this'" Betty then made a gesture as if she was holding something up in her hand the way Abi had that night. "It was that wee thin cheap chain" Betty said with wonderment in her voice.

"I went and woke my Ma up, because I thought it was probably my Ma that took the wean to the toilet and Abi had been too tired to realise it was her granny. But my Ma said no, it wisnae her she had been sound asleep, since her head hit the pillow" Betty paused to tell one of her kids to get the tea on.

"I don't know what happened that night Danny, It's possible the wean moved the chair herself and dreamed the rest, it's possible she found the wee chain during the day and just mixed it into her dream. I don't know. I know that I didnae go near my Ma's for months and I know that I have never stayed there again and never will" Betty said with finality.

I spent the next five or ten minutes laughing at them thinking they could fool me with all this nonsense, I told them how many Levels and Highers I had and that it wisnae so easy to fool me. Betty never wavered from her adamant position that the story as she told it was exactly how it had happened. I eyed her suspiciously looking for any signs of a smirk at the corners of her mouth, there were none.

It was another week or two just before Christmas before I heard the next wee story, we were visiting Patricia's aunt Doris at Patricia's granny's house. Her aunt Doris lived in Lincoln but was through to see her Ma and Da for a couple of days before she would go back to Lincoln on Christmas Eve.

Patricia was right I did like her aunt Doris, she was a lovely wee cuddly woman with a big generous smile, there was something a wee bit sad about her smile it never quite lit up her eyes, but I found out why.

Patricia's Granny's house was in McLean square, they were new houses that were built when Mclean street got knocked down a few years before. It was strange for me because her granny's house was almost exactly on the spot where our house had been on Mclean street before we had moved to Cessnock. I looked out of the living room window and had almost the same view that we had from our kitchen window in the tenement flat we lived in all those years ago.

I touched the back of my head and fingered a scar that ran along the top of my neck. I got that scar when they knocked the old tenements down, it was about two years after we had moved out. I would have eleven or twelve. Charlie had told me the old houses were all getting knocked down and that we should go and watch because there would probably be a rats flitting.

A rat's flitting is a phenomenon seen in the streets around the docks in Glasgow. I don't know why, I'm not David Attenborough, but every so often a streets entire population of rats would move to another street. I had seen it once when I was about six, I had stood at a bedroom window with two of my brothers watching as thousands upon thousands of rats came out of closes, down drainpipes up through the street drains and virtually cover the entire street with their black bristly bodies, squirming all over each other. The one I had seen when I was six had gone on for twenty two minutes, Dunky had stood there timing it, and I could still remember him continually saying that's fourteen minutes that's twenty minutes.

As it turned out there wasn't a rats flitting when they knocked the McLean street down just a lot of rubble and dust and a bit of slate which flew across the street, right at me and went over my head and exploded against the wall I was leaning on. A shard of that slate embedded itself in the back of my head just where it joins my neck and I ran screaming like wee lassie all the way home. It got twelve stitches and I felt justified in my screaming. Charlie called me Darleney for a few weeks, which was his way of saying that I was like a wee mixture of Danny and Darlene for screaming like a maddie.

Patricia's granny arrived with a tea tray and told me to come away from the window and sit down and have some tea. It was Patricia that said to Doris that I didn't believe the ghost stories about her ma's house and to tell me they were true.

Doris chuckled, and showed her happy side and then said "I don't know if the stories are true or not, I can only tell you what happened to me, and you can judge the truth of it for yourself."

I smiled and said "That sounds fair, go for it"

She smiled again, that enigmatic smile that didn't seem to entirely reach her eyes, it seemed a genuine smile I don't mean to imply it wasn't. There was just something there something preventing her from completing the smile.

She began her tale "I was up in Patricia's ma's house, just visiting it was about tea time, I was starting to think about getting home, to make Jake's dinner, Jake's my man, he's at the pub just now with my Da, you will meet him later" Doris said.

"Anyway, my Christopher's bum was soaking wet and smelled like a Bombay toilet so I thought I better change him before I could think about going anywhere. So I cleared the coffee table in front of the fire and laid out a towel on it and started to change his arse. Jean, Patricia's Ma, came in with a cup of tea for me, but I had put the wean on the coffee table so I told her to put it on the mantelpiece and I would drink it when I was done. So she did, she put it right next to the chair I was sitting on just up above my head." She paused to smile and look at me to see if I was following her story. I was.

"I got on with changing his bum and thought I'll just have a wee sip of that tea before it gets cold. And I reached up behind me but the cup wasn't there. I looked up at the mantelpiece and saw the cup at the other end the window end I could have sworn that Jean had left it at my end, but never mind, I stood up and reached across for it and put it back at my end, I tucked it behind that wee jar she has on her mantelpiece, sugary she calls it. I had a strange thought that I didn't want it sliding down the other end again. But it couldn't have there was a big brass carriage clock right in the middle nothing could have slid past that. It didn't matter Jean must have moved it and I was too busy with Christopher's nappy to notice" When she said the name Christopher again, she glanced at Patricia and Patricia gave her a sympathetic smile, which was a bit odd.

"So I finished cleaning the wee man's bum, slapped some talc on it, wrapped him in a nappy and put his rubbers on. When I lay him down to crawl about I reached up for my tea again and it wisnae where I had put it.

It was back down the other end of the mantelpiece." She said with a told you so expression on her face.

"No way" I said "You're just making that up"

"No I'm not" she said, if you want to accuse me of making something up you would be better accusing me about the last bit Danny, because when I looked along at the cup of tea, it moved along the mantelpiece by itself and went back to where I had left it in the first place. So I am either a nutcase or there was something weird happening, I don't think I'm a nutcase"

Like I had with Betty, I stared at her waiting for her face to twitch or her lip to quiver and for her to admit it was a joke, she didn't. Patricia's granny broke the tension by saying "Take a wee biscuit with your tea Paddy" That was the first time I met Patricia's granny, I probably knew her for twenty years, I held her hand the night she died, she always called me Paddy. No matter how many times I corrected her, I worked out why she did it eventually. She let slip that she knew I had an Irish name and that it was an Irish name in a famous song. But instead of Danny boy, she always thought of Paddy McGinty's goat.

I asked Patricia later about the look of sympathy from her to Doris, she told me that the little boy who's nappy Doris had been changing that night had died just a couple of years before, in a terrible accident. I now knew the reason that Doris's smile couldn't reach all the way to her eyes and my heart wept for her. I remembered my sister Dorothy's pain when she lost wee Daisy, and Daisy was just a wee baby, I could only imagine how much worse it must have been to lose a six year old child. I admired Doris's ability to go on, the strength she must have needed to get through such a devastating ordeal must have been immense.

Christmas was coming so was the New Year, so was our double engagement party, things were a bit hectic to say the least. I bought an engagement ring. Patricia went with me to choose it, I learned a couple of early lessons that helped me for a long time. When Patricia was buying something she started at the top end, the most expensive the most exclusive and then worked her way down to something that was on the very edge of our affordability. The second lesson was that I knew nothing about anything that mattered. I knew nothing about clothes. I knew nothing about jewellery, I knew nothing, absolutely nothing, about shoes and most importantly I knew nothing about women. I was a brand new packet of Plasticine, waiting patiently for someone with wisdom and taste to mould me into a recognisable man shape. The other thing I didn't know was that being moulded was sometimes painful for the Plasticine.

"What about that ring" I asked pointing at the bottom tray in the window which had silver rings priced between ten and twenty pounds.

Patricia looked at me, I think she was trying to work out whether I was joking or not and when she was sure that I wasn't she laughed in my face. "A silver engagement ring, are you serious. Would you like to give me a black eye in time for our engagement party because that would be less embarrassing than a silver engagement ring?"

I scrunched my face up, "That's a bit strong, it was only a suggestion. I once seen somebody with a silver engagement ring on the telly" I said trying to save face.

She smiled at me patiently "No you didnae, you might have seen somebody with a white gold engagement ring, silver engagement rings don't exist. Nobody else in the world is miserable enough to want one" And the pattern of our lives began.

After she had tried on every one of the rings in the five to six hundred pounds range, we settled on one that cost sixty five pounds and we were both sort of happy. She was happy that at least she had a gold ring it was only nine carat but it was gold, and I was glad that I didn't have to spend my entire wealth, which at that point was one hundred and forty pounds on a ring. I suppose the pain of spending just over a week's wages on a ring will leave me eventually.

"What are we going to wear" she asked as we walked away from Ratner's gold shop with the ring tucked away in my trouser pocket.

"What do you mean" I asked naively.

"For the engagement party" she said.

"I gave her a puzzled look, whatever you want, and I'll wear whatever's clean" I said marvelling at her ability to worry over trivial things, why would it matter what we wear we were in my Ma's house, it wasn't as if we were going out or something. And why would anybody in the world think about what to wear to a party two weeks before they were going to it. I asked her that.

"Why are you even thinking about what to wear in two weeks' time" I asked teasing her.

She looked at me as if I was an alien and she couldn't understand a word I was saying, "What do you mean two weeks, I have been thinking about what to wear since the day we decided we were getting engaged, and just so as you know, I've been thinking about my wedding dress since I was five."

"Well I will probably think about what to wear when I wake up the morning of the party" I replied and smiled.

She gave me a look of pure anger. "Does this mean nothing at all to you, we are getting engaged that means we are going to get married, and you don't care what you will be wearing to our engagement party." And then she cried.

I tried to put my arms round her she pushed me away. "If you don't care what you will be wearing that means you don't care about getting engaged and that means you don't care about me" she wailed.

I don't think this was my first encounter with feminine logic, but it was probably the first time I recognised it so clearly. So I was left with a choice, I could reassure her that I cared and calmed her down with a cuddle and some soothing words or I could tell her what I thought were the facts of the matter. Why do I never choose the easy option?

"Don't be so bloody stupid, what has what socks I will be wearing got to do with whether I care about you or not. Do you seriously think anybody except you cares what I wear, do you think your ma will be saying to herself "He's got dirty denims on, he canny think much of my Patricia" do you?" I said exasperated.

64

But I got even more exasperated when she responded "Of course she will, it's not me that's stupid it's you that's stupid if you don't think every woman there will think the same thing, if you look like a tramp it means you don't care about me. And no way will you be wearing dirty denims are you mental"

We were in the middle of Argyle Street and she was now actually shouting at me. I was bamboozled, where had this come from? What had I said to cause this anger? I didn't have a clue.

"Come on we will go and get a cup of tea, and you can calm down." I said and when she flashed me a look of anger I added "We can go into Wimpey's and get a burger as well if you're hungry."
She walked away from me in what I can only describe as a huff, now what had I done?

I caught up with her and walked beside her for a while, leaning in and putting my face in front of hers and smiling. I thought it was romantic and funny, she didn't. "Get away from me, you're an idiot" she said pushing me away and turning back and walking towards where we had just come from. I followed her again, she had tears in her eyes "This is really important to me" I don't want to look like a tramp and I don't want you to look like a tramp, you think it doesn't matter, but I do"

"Ok then, I will get some money, if that's what we need then that's what I will get. But it means you can't have chips with your burger, we need to save up." I said putting my arms around her and kissing the tip of her nose. She hugged me back.

Later that night I was sat at the kitchen table with a notepad and pen, trying to work out the easiest and quickest way to get money. I could sell all my possessions, but I don't think twelve pound fifty was going to help. I was reduced to writing things like watching cars on Saturday when Rangers would be playing, but that meant muscling in on Paul and David, and in a fair fight they could probably beat me. Darlene was down visiting my Ma and was sitting at the other end of the table talking to Patricia.

"Aye you should have seen her face, it was like an ugly twisted mask" Darlene was saying as she screwed up her own face into an ugly grimace.

"Who's face?" I asked, I should have known better than to ask.

"My ma's" she said giving me a look that suggested I was stupid for not realising that's who she was talking about.

"What?" I said astonished, I looked behind me to make sure the kitchen door was closed, my Ma would be hurt if she heard what this halfwit was saying.

"What are you looking at me like that for, her face did look horrible it wisnae her fault it was that celebrity palsy she had" she said to me indignantly.

"What?" I said again, this was getting surreal.

"Are you even denying that she had celebrity palsy then, you know she did, you were there, or was your head stuck in a book as usual and you missed it like you miss most things." She said dismissively.

It took me a minute or more to work out what she was actually saying.

"Darlene, you nut job. It wasn't cerebral palsy it was Bell's palsy, it's a completely different thing. That's a really stupid thing to say cerebral palsy is really really bad. You can be a numpty sometimes honestly" I said going back to my writing pad and wishful thinking about how I would raise money.

Patricia piped up "She never said ceraborial palsy, she said celebrity palsy, when she said that I thought she meant your ma's face was all twisted like Bernie winters or Marty Feldman or somebody"

She was serious, I had a terrible thought. I had fallen in love with a girl who was a carbon copy of my sister, I know we are a close family but that's taking it too far. A shiver ran down my spine when Patricia added "I know you think you are really clever Danny but sometimes you let your brains fill your head"

I was sat staring slack jawed back and forth between the two of them when Charlie burst in with his usual exuberance.

"Alright Patty hen, still struggling to attract a decent boyfriend I see, you should try getting out a bit more" He said heading, as usual, straight for the fridge, and devouring a full packet of boiled ham and a pint of milk in seconds.

"Go and make us a couple of pieces and sausage Danny boy, I'm starving." He said, throwing a packet of square sliced on the table.

"Why me" I asked "There's two women sitting here and you ask me, why not them, and don't call her Patty her name's Patricia" I said petulantly.

"Because Darlene couldn'y fry a sausage to save her life, and if Patricia gets up to make it then I get deprived of sitting here and looking at her lovely face, I can live without looking at your face for five minutes" he beamed his trademark grin and Patricia fell for it.

What am I saying? I fell for it as well and made him his pieces and sausage. When he finished eating he picked up my note pad and ushered me out to the hall, saying we had man business to talk about.

"Patricia told Iris you'se two are struggling for money, for Christmas and the engagement party and that, is this you writing out your plan to get money." He asked waving the notepad at me.

When I looked at him with anger he didn't give me a chance to reply before he said "Here, ma and Searcher did a wee job at the weekend" he said and handed me a wee tight roll of what looked like ten pound notes.

I looked at him and at the money in my hand and realised he had put me in another dilemma which is what he was best at.

"What job" I asked.

He smiled at me, "Danny, why do you always ask questions that you don't really want the answer to, go in and give Patricia some money to get something nice to wear and then get her a nice Christmas present, she's a lovely looking wee thing and well out of your league but if you keep her sweet you might get away with it and we can all live happily ever after. Or

67

you can be all high and mighty and tell me to stick my dirty money up my Jacksie and be a wee twat."

"What job?" I asked again.

He laughed and grabbed me round the neck pulling me down until my head was under his arm "We nicked a van full of plumbing stuff and sold it straight away, there were no grannies and no kittens harmed in getting our hands on all this dirty money." He laughed again rapped his knuckles on the top of my head and let me go. I stood up straight and looked him right in the eye, he just smirked gave me a double handed slap on the cheeks and left, chuckling to himself.

I counted the cash, there was two hundred and fifty quid. Did I care where it had come from? Yes and no, yes because I am a terrible worrier with a conscience. No I didn't really care because whatever had happened had already happened and I couldn't change it. I knew this was a pathetic get out clause but so what nobody's perfect.

"Do you fancy going shopping tomorrow" I said to Patricia, dropping fifteen of the tenners onto the table in front of her. She looked at it all doe eyed, like butter wouldn't melt.

"Of course I do, what are we shopping for" she asked, not where did you get that, or why have you got that when you were skint earlier today.

"Something to wear at our engagement party for both of us and whatever we can get for Christmas presents" I said smiling. She jumped up and kissed me and said "What time does What Every Woman Wants open on a Sunday" Paul had just walked into the kitchen as I mentioned Christmas presents and he said "I want a Showaddywaddy suit and a pair of brothel creepers"
I just looked at him with surprise and said "Are you even twelve yet, why do you want some old guys gear, do you want a nice tank top as well like Donnie and my Da?"

"Would that be instead of the wank tops that you wear" he said which got him and David rolling about on the floor laughing, the wee shites had no respect for me at all. Patricia didn't help when she joined in with their laughter.

## Chapter  20. Engagements, Births and near death experiences.

"Why do they call it getting engaged" David asked me, he was sitting on the toilet, I was in the bath. I hadn't invited him in, as a matter of fact I had locked the door and told him repeatedly to piss off he could do the toilet when I was finished having a bath. Dunky helpfully kicked the door in for him and told him "There you go wee man, go and fill the toilet and make it as smelly as you can and that will teach Danny the Fanny not to lock you out when you are bursting for a shit" I missed Dunky when he was away, the level of conversation always dipped. I grabbed one of those checked face cloths that my Ma kept on the wee plastic shelf thing across the bath to cover myself up.

"How should I know" I shouted at him, David was nine or ten, the same age as his and my nephews Mark and wee Tony, but he was at least twelve times as irritating as the other two put together. As it was the New Year, those two would be here as well, Dorothy was through, just for the weekend and Donnie had brought wee Mark and Maggie down to my Ma's because Annie had been taken into hospital that morning with labour pains. Their other two wee Duncan and wee Charlie were with some of Annie's family. Donnie had intended just staying at our house until the bells, he reckoned the hospital would phone if there was any news and since Annie already had four weans, he didn't think she would be that bothered if he was there or not. My Ma and Dorothy hounded him out of the door to the hospital.

"But, that's what it says on the door of a toilet when there's somebody in, engaged. So why do they call having a girlfriend being engaged, does that mean that you and Charlie and Iris and Patricia will be like a locked door where nobody else can get in. Like when you widnae let me in earlier before Dunky kicked the door in" the stupid wee brat asked me.

"Will you just do your shite and beat it?" I asked ducking my head under the water, I only lasted a couple of minutes before I had to come up for air. He was rocking back and forward laughing, and throwing out a couple of farts for good measure, he still had his trousers and pants round his ankles and his arse inside the toilet pan, it must have been nearly in the water the way he was sitting.

"Do a shite and beat it, you said, did you mean beat it like an egg" he couldn't contain himself he thought he was that funny.

"David, I swear to god, I will strangle you and hide you up in the shelf in the coal bunker, it's the New Year, nobody will notice you are missing or even care that you are missing for about a week, I will get away with it, and I will tell you something nobody will even care, because you are the most annoying irritating little bast.."

I was interrupted by Darlene "Are you nearly done" she asked, as she walked straight into the bathroom and checked her hair in the mirror.

"Did you not even shut the door you manky wee bast...."

This time I was interrupted by Dorothy walking into the bathroom "Have you seen my mascara Darlene, you better not have touched it that cost me two quid it's not one of your cheap Woolworths rubbish, it was out of Boots" she said elbowing Darlene aside, and looking in the bathroom cabinet.

I shouted, "No, I'm not nearly finished I just got in this bath will you'se all please get out I am trying to have a bath for my engagement party tonight."

Dorothy laughed and said "Are you gonny have a bath every time you get engaged or is this one special" and left giggling to herself like an eejit.

Darlene said, "I wisnae talking to you, I was talking to him, are you nearly finished" she said pointing at David.

"Aye" he said, and stood up and pulled his pants and trousers up.

"Euuggh" Darlene said "You never even wiped your arse and look at that big log you left in the toilet" as she boaked and pulled the cistern chain at the same time. "Nae wonder your pants are all skid marks you dirty wee article" She called after David as he slipped out of the room but not before splashing my bath water in my face as he left.

And just as I though it couldn't get any worse she turned round took her pants down without lifting her skirt the way girls can do and sat down and had a pee. I started screaming for my Ma. I wished we had a bigger coal bunker. After Darlene had left, I leapt out and locked the door behind her covering my modesty with the wet facecloth, just before I could Charlie nipped in. He started stripping off.

"What are you doing, you must be joking" I said.

"I might as well get in beside you Danny, we are never both going to have time for a bath" he actually dropped his trousers and pants before I had a chance to stop him and slid into the bath.

"Water's a bit cold Danny, top up the hot a wee bit eh?" he laughed and added "It's been ages since we shared a bath Danny, get yourself in, you look freezing standing there"

"This is a fuckin madhouse" I said and started just having a wash at the sink

So that was me had my bath then, I chose to dry myself off and get dressed in the comfort and privacy of my own bedroom.

"What are you doing in here Dorothy and why are you standing in your knickers and that ridiculously big bra" I asked with exasperation, as I opened my bedroom door.

"This is my room for the weekend, and if you don't get out I will take the ridiculously big bra off and frighten you to death, now go away" she said, quite reasonably I suppose.

I stood outside my own bedroom door, "Can I at least get some clothes out of my wardrobe, it's nearly ten o'clock and Patricia and her maw will be here shortly, my clothes for tonight are all on one hanger in my wardrobe. Patricia picked them out for me and ironed them all last night. If I don't wear them tonight she will probably tell me to stick my ring where the sun doesn't shine" I said pleadingly.

Dot opened the door and dragged me in by the arm. "She picked what you have to wear? Are you having a laugh? Who does she think she is? Who does she think you are, her wee ken that she can take out of his box and just dress up when it suits her?" she rattled off question after question, I don't think she actually expected me to answer any of them, she was just enjoying having a moan I think.

"Who's Ken" I asked.

"Barbie" she answered with an accusing look on her face.

"What?" I asked, immediately feeling guilty, if Dot was looking at me accusingly, it was probably because I had done something. Even though I couldn't remember actually doing anything I must have, or she wouldn't be accusing me of it. She always knew when I did something wrong even why I didn't. Her look reminded me of an incident when I was only about nine or ten.
Dot had sent me to Mr Patel's on Christmas day to get her some cigarettes, she had given me a fiver and told me to get forty Benson & Hedges, which were about sixty pence a packet. So she should have got about three pounds eighty change, I gave her about one pound seventy.

"Where's the rest?" She asked when I handed her the money.

"That's all he gave me" I said with guilt written all over my face.

"Where's the rest of my change Danny" She asked again, coldly.

I panicked, I should have told the truth right there and then, and I could have escaped with some dignity at least. "That's what he gave me" I tried again. She sat up, she had been lying on the couch watching some Christmas film. It was unusual for anybody to get to lie down on the couch in our house, I think she was so short and wide that she took up the same room lying down as she did sitting up and that's why she got away with it

72

and no one else did, she could lie on the couch and there would still be room for at least two others to sit down, and of course that she would just batter anybody other than my Ma or Da who objected.

"Danny, Mr Patel's got a new one armed bandit in his shop, is the rest of my change in that machine" she asked, with her normal all-knowing wisdom. That was my second chance to admit that I had put the biggest part of her change in the puggie. I didn't take it. I decided to stick to the story that I had been short changed. There was no way she was going to go to the shop to check, it was Christmas day and it was freezing.

"David throw me my slippers over son, I need to go and get my money back from that thieving bastard Mr Patel." She again looked at me with disbelief that I was going to make her go through with this charade. That was the third and last chance she gave me to escape my stupidity.

I still didn't take it. It was only when she had actually got up put her slippers and a coat on and basically dragged me across the road to Mr Patel's that I relented slightly.

"Maybe I dropped it" I said, tearfully.

"She looked at me and said "And maybe you need to learn that lying is worse than stealing" and dragged me into the shop.

"Hello harry, how are you and how is Meena" Dot said to Mr Patel, who was smiling.

"I am very well Dorothy, and Meena is still beautiful and lovely fat" He wagged his head from side to side, made an hourglass figure with his hands and laughed, Dot laughed with him. Meena is his wife and she is fat.

"How much did Danny put in this puggie Mr Patel" Dorothy asked him, without any more small talk or preamble.

Mr Patel looked at me with sympathy and said "Two pounds, it was, twice I made change for a pound note for him. Sorry Danny"

Dorothy grabbed me by the collar of my shirt and virtually dragged me the whole way home, across the Zebra crossing over Paisley Road and down Cessnock Street and up the close stairs. She let go of me when we were in the hall, and she slapped me right across the face. "If you ever want something from me you can have it, whatever it is. But don't steal from me Danny and don't ever lie to me. I can't take that son. Go to bed." I never did, again.

As this memory flashed through my mind, I was still trying to work out what I had done this time.
"What?" I asked again, grinning now because I knew I hadn't actually done anything.

"Is she a nice lassie Danny?" she asked with seriousness in her voice.

"Who?" I asked mischievously.

"The young Diana Dors, you're getting engaged to, you know who, don't be wide. Is she a nice lassie Danny?" she said again, she stared straight into my eyes watching for the truth.

"I love her Dot, she's a great lassie, really innocent and good, I'm going to look after her. She needs me to look after her." I said matching her seriousness, although it was difficult standing dripping wet with only a towel round me practically freezing to death.

"Does she love you Danny?" Dorothy asked.

"What's that got to do with anything Dot? I love her that's all that matters, I don't need to be loved, I've got my Ma and all of you'se for that. She thinks she disnae have anybody that loves her, but I do, I love her and I will show her." I said smiling. Dot grabbed me and pulled my head down to her level and kissed me, and all she said was "Okay"

"Can I get my clothes then?" I asked, she nodded and I went in to get them. As I turned round to leave the room with them she put her hands behind her back as if to undo her bra strap. I screamed like a little girl and ran "What's the matter with my sisters, all they want to do is take their boobs out and scare people with them" I shouted as I scurried across to Paul's room to get dressed, trying to carry all my clothes, my shoes, and hold up the towel around my waist.

I am not sure why I was getting so excited, it was only Patricia and her ma that were coming tonight, I felt all nervous and sweaty. It was the first time my Ma would meet her Ma but that wouldn't be a big deal would it?

She arrived just after ten o'clock and she looked beautiful, she always looked beautiful but she was stunning tonight in a gypsy skirt and a silky top which she described as off the shoulder. Her ma looked a bit nervous surrounded by McCallister's, but trust my Da he was right in there turning on the charm, getting her a drink getting her a comfortable seat but not before he waltzed her across the living room floor just because a waltz tune came on the telly as they went in the living room. Patricia's Ma giggled like a wee lassie and I am sure she blushed a wee bit, nice one Da.

I got Patricia and her Ma a drink, her Ma said Patricia could have a shandy since it was the New Year but no more than that. I was forgetting that Patricia was only sixteen. It was easy for me to forget particularly as we had been out the night before and both of us had been steaming and ended up in my bed all night.

I sneaked Patricia out of the living room and into the kitchen as soon as I thought it would go unnoticed, her ma was busy getting schmoozed by my Da and my Ma was busy keeping an eye on my Da in case he went too far, which he could, and Dot was busy keeping an eye on my Ma so she didn't have a jealous wobbly like she sometimes could if my Da was paying too much attention to another woman. I had never really noticed the undercurrents of jealousy in my family before but it appeared to be raising its ugly head quite a lot recently. It had always been there of course I had just been too young to either see it or recognise it for what it was but I was getting the picture now.

We were stood by the kitchen sink I had my arms around her waist she had her arms around my neck, we were kissing. "Let's forget this party and just go to bed" I whispered in her ear, we couldn't stand at the sink any longer, I was far too excited.

"No way" she said but continued kissing me and talking in between kisses "This is our engagement party, we canny just disappear"

I smirked and said "What I've got in mind is to disappear or maybe just stay right here, or to tell the truth what I've got in mind is making love to you"

She pushed me away giggling, "That's Billie Jo Spears' song, don't be stupid"

"I think maybe you should go and find where Billie Jo Spears lives, because if that's what you have in mind you're not going near my Patricia" her Ma said as she was stood near the kitchen door.

I was facing Patricia with my back to her Ma I felt an uncontrollable urge to laugh Patricia was looking at me as if to say, don't you dare. I didn't laugh but when I said without turning round "Would it be at least alright Mrs Miller if I took her to a small café out of the way." We both burst out laughing, her Ma didn't, at first but eventually broke a smile.

"Both of you, in the living room and I will be watching, so no sneaking out when I'm not looking, and you lady will be coming home with me tonight. I'm still not sure I believe that you stayed at your sisters last night, I will be asking her when I see her." Her Ma said and wandered away, I am sure she was only looking for the toilet.
"Will Betty back you up" I asked "you're not going to get in to bother for this are you?"

"I don't know and I don't care" Patricia answered me "I'm sixteen I can do what I want, we are getting engaged and gonny get married what we do is our business and it's too late for her to kid on she cares, earlier on the day she was sitting drinking with two of her sisters, my auntie Doris and auntie Sarah. I begged her not to get drunk, that we were coming here tonight and I didn't want to be embarrassed if she was steaming and falling all over the place. But she did it anyway I got home at about five o'clock with my pals from McCulloch street, Jackie and Samantha. Samantha might come down later by the way I gave her your address." She paused for breath, this was all interesting but I had something else in mind rather than hearing about her ma being drunk, but I knew I had to let her get this off her ample chest or she wouldn't entertain what I had in mind.

"So anyway me and Jackie and Sam get in the house and there's my Ma singing crying time again and giving it laldy with Doris. I screamed at her you're not going to my engagement party. You're nothing but an old drunk. But Sam and Jackie are all over her making her cups of black coffee and running her a cold bath and all that sobering her up. That's why we never got here till after ten o'clock, she's still half drunk, did you no see her staggering across the floor, with your Da he had to practically hold her up." She paused again, I was kind of hoping that was the end of her story so we could move on to my plan, but it wasn't.

"She does this to me all the time, if it was her precious son Robert's engagement she widnae be steaming in the afternoon before it, aw naw she would be right prim and proper and respectable." She ranted.

I took the slight opportunity she had given me and butted in. "She isnae actually steaming, and she wisnae staggering that was my Da dragging her about, he does the same to my Ma but she is really quick with her wee tiny feet so it looks as if they are dancing, if My Da disnae dance with my Ma he looks like a big haddie, it's only her that makes him look good"

She looked puzzled as she asked "Why are you talking about your Ma and Da dancing, I was talking about my Ma being an old drunk and you better watch her with your Da, she isnae fussy who she goes with when she's drunk, and don't make excuses for her she is drunk I can tell."

I didn't know whether to be offended for my Da or not but I had bigger fish to fry. "You know how you said we can do what we want" I asked her as I pulled her close and kissed her.

"Aye we can do what we want and she won't stop us, that's for sure" Patricia said vehemently.

"If we can do what we want why don't we just go to bed then" I asked plaintively. Ignoring everything else she had just said.

"We can do what we want, not just what you want" she said then smiled her beautiful smile and kissed me "Although I want that as well as it goes" she said and kissed me like she meant it. So we did but we weren't that tired and got back up after half an hour for the bells.

"3-2-1 happy new year" Charlie shouted and sprayed a can of Kestrel lager about the living room as if it was a bottle of champagne.

"You are an idiot" Darlene screamed at him. "it cost me four quid to get this French toast put in my hair" Patricia whispered to me "Does she mean French bun" I shrugged my shoulder's, how should I know what Darlene meant, if she didn't know what she meant how could anybody else. Patricia's pal Samantha turned up after the bells. She was Patricia's best pal but not really my cup of tea. She spent ten minutes telling me how Patricia's first love had been her brother Johnnie and how they had been inseparable for years, and how she thought that they would probably get married and she would be Patricia's bridesmaid. The way she made it sound I was surprised she never mentioned the wee white country cottage they would all live in happily ever after. This Johnnie sounded like a right prick. There's that jealousy again.

Samantha then spent the next half an hour flirting with me, I know I think lassies are always after me, well she wisnae really after me but she was flirting with me, trying to make Patricia jealous I suppose. She stopped it quite quickly when I said to her "Look how lovely Patricia's blonde hair is when the lights shine on it, and look out how lovely and slim she is, would you no like to be that slim" It was an innocent question there was no need for her to take the huff the way she did.

Not long after the bells Dunky came in and turned the music down, which was a pity because somebody had just put Dr Hook's album on. "Listen everybody, Donnie just phoned, Annie has had a wee girl and they are calling her Mary Jane" Dunky announced and Charlie took a second opportunity to spray some Kestrel lager round the room, this time a can he had a can in each hand.

The rest of the night went great, Patricia's Ma was the life and soul, she indulged in a very enthusiastic version of the twist with Tony, Dot's husband, and anybody who could keep up with him had to go some, he danced like a scarecrow with bees in his pants. She also joined in the sing song with just as much enthusiasm as she danced. Unfortunately for her there were a lot of fine chanter's in our house and she wisnae quite up to their standard but she made up for lack of talent with loudness. Dot was the star turn she sang I'm gonna sit right down and write myself a letter, which brought the house down' then Donnie who had just arrived back from the hospital looking knackered sang love letters in the sand, he wisnae the best but he was alright. Dunky did a good version of Wild Rover, a clean version. I kept singing the choruses I knew from when I played rugby and Patricia elbowed me in the ribs every time I did. My ma had once told me that I sometimes opened my mouth and let everything out whether it annoyed or hurt anybody or not, maybe Patricia was going to be my filter, I hoped so.

Charlie started to sing the soldier song, a Celtic football song but was shouted down, with cries of no party songs, I never did understand why Rangers and Celtic songs were described as party songs, I don't think I ever went to a party in my life where they were allowed to be sung.

The party went on until it got light which must have been about half eight in the morning, well it went on much longer than that. It actually slowed down for most of the morning but then kicked back up again when a couple of my Da's brothers arrived with their families in the afternoon fully laden with dozens of cans of Tennent's lager, a bottle of Bell's whisky for my Da and a bottle of Bristol Cream for my Ma. I didn't see any of that, when my Da's brothers arrived in a taxi, I commandeered it and took Patricia her mum and Samantha home to Pollokshields. Samantha spent the journey glaring at me, and Patricia spent the journey glaring at me, because she was wondering what I had done to Samantha to make her glare at me, Patricia's Ma spent the journey snoring and slobbering down her chin, she was steaming now alright' and it wasn't a pretty sight.

We spent the morning sleeping and the afternoon visiting some of Patricia's pals in McCulloch Street, I got to meet Samantha's brother Johnnie Boyle, Patricia's ex. I bristled a bit, being a McCallister I then metaphorically beat my chest and marked my territory but there was no real need, Patricia had told me that they had been boyfriend and girlfriend but it was when they were kids. By the strangest coincidence Johnnie Boyle was now engaged to a girl who had lived at the end of Cessnock Street, Roberta Rankin. We didn't stay long at the Boyle's, long enough to meet the father of the family a great big guy with a resounding Irish accent, a great character that I would come to like and respect even during the periods when Johnnie and I didn't quite see eye to eye. We didn't stay very long because Patricia wanted to take me around a few of her friends, hopefully she was showing me off. McCulloch Street was very similar to Cessnock Street in that it resembled a village where everybody knew everybody else's business. Quite a few of the people we met already knew who I was because they knew who Charlie was, due to him being a frequent visitor and they had noticed me on the few occasions that I had visited Patricia over the past few months.

By tea time we had met a good few people and I was getting a reasonably good feeling about the place, which was good because we were going to spend the next eighteen years of our lives living there. We headed back to Cessnock Street to my house to find that a party was still in full swing neither of us fancied it so we trudged back up to McCulloch Street, which was a good forty five minute walk.

Patricia's Ma was up and about by the time we got there, although she was walking about like a half shut knife, I never knew this but apparently too much whisky could give you a sore back. We sat with her for a while as she watched some film called Dr Shivago and must have fell asleep about twenty times through it. Eventually Patricia persuaded her to go to bed.

"Is he staying?" her Ma asked pointing at me.

"Don't be so rude Ma, no he isnae" Patricia said and looked at me, I must have looked disappointed, because she said "Unless he wants to" looking at me for a decision. Of course I wanted to was she mental?

"If you don't mind Mrs Miller I can sleep anywhere, on the couch or on the floor, I could with no having to walk back down to Cessnock and I canny afford a taxi, I spent the last of my money on that taxi we got this morning." I said trying to incite some guilt on her part for letting me pay all the taxi fare earlier on.

"Well you certainly won't be sleeping in Patricia's room, there will be none of that hanky panky under my roof. You are only engaged not married." She said haughtily.

I didn't yet know my possible future mother in law very well, but Patricia had told me a few little facts over the months we had been going out.

80

Facts like her Ma had had four children, all with different fathers and at least one or two had been born out of wedlock. In fact her eldest daughter Betty, the one who Patricia was staying with in Lambhill Street was brought up as her sister. Which was a very frequent occurrence in Glasgow at the time. In fact our big rivals in Cessnock Street the Watsons did the exact same thing but the youngster didn't find out until she was in her mid-twenties and all hell let loose.

So I was a bit sceptical of her moral stance about not sleeping in Patricia's room, but then she said something which still makes me laugh today.

"Since you two are engaged, I will let you put Patricia's single mattress down on the floor behind the sofa, she can sleep on that and you can sleep on the couch. But only if you promise to stay on the couch all night" she looked at me seriously as if she expected me to take an oath, I didn't know whether to laugh or cross my heart and hope to die.

"Of course I will stay on the couch Mrs Miller, I widnae dream of doing anything that would upset you in your own house" I said with the sweetest smile I could manage. How crazy was she? I was eighteen years old, I had just, the night before, got engaged to a sixteen year old girl who could only be described as sex on legs. And she expected me to sleep on a couch just eighteen inches away from where this goddess, who, by the way wanted me, was sleeping. Aye right Mrs Miller okay then.

Approximately four minutes after we heard her Ma flush the toilet and shut her bedroom door behind her, Patricia said to me "I'm a bit cold down here on the floor by myself" less than one second after that I was lying beside her heating her up.

After we had got heated up, which we had to do twice because the first time we got too hot too fast and kicked the quilt off so we had to get heated up all over again but we took our time that time. We were lying there in the semi dark having a smoke, the only light was from the electric fire which was a one bar fire, because that's all Mrs Miller said she could afford to burn. But it was a nice wee glow, I finished my fag and snuggled in behind Patricia while she finished hers.

I started to sort of doze off and was woken by Patricia stretching across me to put her cigarette out in an ashtray which was at my side of the

81

mattress on the floor. Or at least that's what I thought was happening when I opened my eyes, there was someone kneeling over me but it Wasn't Patricia. It was an extremely old woman with white straggly hair and not a single tooth in her head. She moved her face towards me and I smelled a stench like an open sewer.  In fact that's not quite right, I had smelled a smell like this before. It was outside a butchers shop on Paisley road west, there was a huge open back lorry and the butcher was throwing what looked like pig and cow carcasses onto the back of it.

That's what this old woman smelled like rotten meat that had been left too long in a warm room. I panicked, I grabbed this old woman by the throat with both hands and started to choke her. I could see her eyes bulging, she grabbed at my wrists trying to free herself and shook me from side to side. My head was turned away from her to avoid the stench, when I looked back she had gone. It wasn't her I was choking it was Patricia.

I let her neck go and sat up with my back against the back of the couch, stunned for a few seconds and then I pulled her towards me, almost sobbing how sorry I was. Patricia obviously got a hell of a fright and was being quietly hysterical. Bizarrely we were both whispering, I don't know if that was so as not to disturb her Ma or not to disturb whatever else was there with us.

"I'm sorry I'm sorry, I'm sorry. Oh Patricia baby I'm sorry I' sorry, I'm sorry. I don't know what happened I'm sorry I'm sorry" I was saying, babbling almost.

"Okay, okay, okay Danny it's okay. Tell me what happened but calm down you are scaring me." She whispered in my ear and soothed me. She was holding on to me with an iron grip with one arm around the back of my shoulders and stroking my face with her other hand. I was breathing quite heavily.

"You, you, you were an old woman. You, you, had no teeth and white hair. And I don't know if you were trying to kiss me or bite me but you leaned right into my face." I said breathlessly.

She giggled, not quite the reaction I had expected to be honest. "If I had no teeth how was I going to bite you, did you think I was going to rip open your throat with my gums" and she giggled again.

This calmed me down, "Be serious" I said "I could have choked you to death there, you wouldn't have been giggling then would you, that wouldn't have tickled your funny bone would it" I said and started tickling her ribs. This made her laugh out loud, which wasn't ideal in the circumstances.

"Shush" I said "You will waken that old woman up again" and just as I finished saying that he Ma called out. "Patricia, what's going on in there, that Danny better still be on that bloody couch, don't make me get up and check. Which made us both laugh, but we did our best to keep the laughter in but it tried to erupt out of us, not just through our mouths but through our noses as well. I was spluttering away and Patricia leapt up and said "Oh mammy daddy, I think I might pee myself and rushed out of the living room and into the loo, slamming the door behind her.

I leapt up on to the couch anticipating what was going to happen next and I was right.

"What's all this bloody noise about" Mrs Miller said as she turned the living room light on.

I poked my head out of the quilt I had hurriedly pulled over me just seconds before, rubbed my eyes theatrically and in my best sleepy voice asked "What's the matter Mrs Miller, where's Patricia? Is everything okay, what's all the banging about"

Patricia emerged from the loo and asked why everybody was up, she had got up for a pee and then her ma's bedroom door slamming shut and her Ma start shouting. Her ma looked from me to Patricia and back again. She looked as if she knew something was going on but not exactly what it was.

"Get back on that mattress and both of you get to sleep, I'm starting to think it wisnae a good idea to let you'se two sleep in here together, there is far too much bloody carrying on if you ask me." She pulled her powder blue winter housecoat around her and went back to her room. Patricia leapt on top of me on the couch and we both stuck our heads under the quilt trying to stifle our laughter.

That was the first personal involvement I had with the supposed haunted house at one hundred and fifteen McCulloch Street. I personally think there is always an explanation for ghostly happenings and haunting stories. Let me explain what I think happened that night.

Firstly I was aware of the reputation of the house, I was also in a semi sleepy state. We had been up all night the night before and only grabbed a few hours sleep on Patricia's Ma's couch earlier that morning. So in reality I had probably had three hours sleep in the last forty eight hours. As I said we were on a mattress behind the sofa, the sofa had legs so there was maybe a six inch gap below the sofa which let the light from the one bar electric fire cast a glow in our faces if we turned towards the fire, even lying on the mattress like we were.

So there I was lying there half asleep, I think, when Patricia leaned over me to stub out her fag, the firelight would have been casting shadows and flickers on her face. I woke up and saw these shadows and flickers and somehow my semi -awake brain translated them as the face of an old woman. When I then choked that old woman and sort of pushed her out of the flickering lights, I immediately realised that it was Patricia, and I let her go. The only thing I have never been able to explain to my own satisfaction is the stench. Patricia likes to tell me that I must have farted with fear when I thought her Ma had got into bed with us, because sometimes apparently my farts smell like rotting meat.

I don't know for sure what happened that night, I think my explanation to myself is reasonable. I do know that I never felt comfortable in that attic ever again. There were other events which cemented my unease with that house, which I will tell you about in good time.

Over the next couple of months I virtually moved in with Patricia and her mum. Not officially but I spent more time there than I did in my own house. Her Ma persisted with making me sleep on the couch and Patricia on the mattress behind the couch. I have never found out if she did that in a genuine belief that we stayed apart during the night or if it was just to kid herself on that she had done all she could to prevent us sleeping together. There was a problem which developed over those months though a problem for me.

When I stayed at Patricia's it was very difficult for me to get to work in Hillington, I started at eight in the morning so I had to get a bus at half seven at the Paisley road toll or I would be late. The paisley Road Toll was a good twenty minute walk or a good ten minute run for me. So when I set my alarm clock, which I now carried about with me because I was never sure where I would be sleeping on any given night. I would set it for half six, the theory being, get up quick cup of tea, quick wash and bolt down to the toll, before half seven and Hamish is your uncle.

That was a good theory, in fact a fine theory, but it had some flaws when put into practice. It was a freezing cold winter, I was eighteen. I was waking up with the most beautiful girl in the world in my arms, and she was warm. In fact she was hot. So three or four days a week in March I was late and in April that turned into two or three days a week I was off sick. That didn't go down well with my employer, it actually went down very very badly with my employer, who was not only paying me a weekly wage, they were also paying my way through my city and guilds course at Cardonald College.

I knuckled down in May and stayed at my Ma's house most of the week and only stayed at Patricia's at the weekends. In June employers dropped a bombshell on me. They were closing the factory in Hillington and transferring all the production to their factory in Swansea. Surprisingly they asked me if I wanted to transfer with them and live in Swansea. They would help me to find rented accommodation or perhaps even help me with a subsidised mortgage for a few years, they were doing this with some senior staff and engineers and had extended this offer to apprentices at the behest of the unions.

I asked Patricia if she fancied it, she said she didn't really but that if I did she would go with me and try it. I said no. the company then made an arrangement with another factory on the estate to allow me to finish my apprenticeship with them since I only had a couple of months to go, until the end of my first Scotvec course which would lead to my city and guilds.

So that was that, I was paid up until Glasgow fair Friday after which I would be out of a job and married because Glasgow fair Friday was our wedding day, och well at least there was no problems with time off for the honeymoon.

Also in early June, Patricia's Ma took me with her into the West of Scotland housing association's offices at Anderson cross and helped me to get a house from them. Which was in McCulloch Street would you believe, number one hundred and one, ground floor first left. It was a room and kitchen, but it was a huge living room and a huge kitchen. I signed a missive, but we wouldn't get the keys until the end of September because the house was being gutted and refurbished.

So there we were, it was the end of June, and we were getting married in less than three weeks, the eighteenth of July to be exact. And I had four weeks wages in my pocket which we were about to spend on the wedding, Patricia had a fulltime job in the bingo, which paid peanuts, But the very day after our wedding day I would be unemployed, but we would have a house with rent to be paid and bills to be paid. We never knew what we had let ourselves in for but we were happy, we really were, but it was the happiness of innocent children.

## Chapter twenty one. Weddings, and our very first house

It was two weeks before the wedding, I would have said everything was organised, apparently I was totally wrong.

"I don't know ask my Ma" I said to Patricia, she was asking who was ordering the buttonholes for the men, I didn't even have a clue what a buttonhole is, I thought it was a hole for a button. Turns out it's the flower that men put on their jackets.

"That's all you ever say, I don't know ask my Ma, I thought it was us organising this wedding not your Ma" Patricia said, with an annoyed tone.

I put David's beano annual down and asked her "What's up with you, everything's sorted by now is it not?"

She burst into tears, Darlene walked into the kitchen in my Ma's, where we were sitting and asked "What's the matter with her now"

"What do you mean 'now'?" I asked her "You are making out that there's always something wrong with her, why don't you keep your nose out for a change" I said at Darlene tetchily.

"I am sitting here, you know, what is it with you McCallister's. You'se all just talk amongst yourselves as if nobody else matters. I matter, and I'm sitting here if you'se didnae notice" Patricia said.

"Who's rattled her cage" Charlie asked when he came into the kitchen, and he fully deserved the tirade of abuse that Patricia launched at him. Although I did feel the smallest amount of sympathy when she eventually stopped shouting at him and stormed out of the kitchen with a parting shot at him "I thought you were alright Charlie but you are just as bad as your bloody sisters"

"And what does she mean by that exactly? Darlene shouted and launched herself at the kitchen door presumably meaning to have it out with Patricia. She was stopped in her tracks by my Ma who told her unsympathetically to sit down and shut up. Dunky then walked in and asked "What's up with Calimero, is she pregnant"

If I hadn't been so worried about Patricia I would have found that quite funny, because Dunky had been calling Patricia, Calimero for months. Calimero was a wee cartoon character, I think it was like a wee Spanish sparrow that had just been born and it wore half of its shell on its head like a hat. The reason he called Patricia after this little bird was because of its catchphrase, it spent all of its time wandering around saying "It's an injustice, it's an injustice" in a wee squeaky voice and Patricia did have a very quiet voice at that time and a habit of saying to me "But Danny that's no fair" Whenever I said she couldn't have something or we couldn't do something. "But Danny that's no fair" was turned into "It's an injustice" every time she said it now either by me or by Dunky.

But Patricia was too upset for me to appreciate Dunkys joke at the time. "Don't call her that and no, she's not pregnant, you're thinking of your own wedding" I said cruelly and unnecessarily.

"That's enough Danny go and settle Patricia down, she's just a bit nervous about the wedding. And when you have bring her back ben here and bring one of your note pads, we can make a wee list of everything and put her mind at ease. It's no wonder the lassie's upset, you'se two are useless" my Ma said indicating Charlie and me. "You'se have left everything to me to organise and the lassie's will be feeling left out, is iris no the same as Patricia, Charlie?" She asked, he just shrugged his shoulder and mumbled something like "Don't know, don't care" through the piece and cheese he was eating.

I went into my bedroom slowly as this was where Patricia had fled in her temper tantrum, although I knew better than to describe it as that. She was lying on her stomach facing away from me towards the window. I could hear her gently sniffling having obviously been crying. I climbed onto the bed slowly and put my arm around her, and kissed the back of her head and ran my hand gently up and down her back trying to sooth her.

"I'm sorry" I said.

"Are you?"

"Aye"

"What for?"

"Eh?"

"What are you sorry for?" she said with a tone of voice I recognised, she was trying to trap me, I thought before answering but obviously I didn't think hard or long enough.

"Everything" I said "I'm sorry you got upset and I'm sorry you're crying" which I thought was fair enough and covered everything.

"So you're not actually sorry then" she said with an attitude.

"Eh?" I said with fear, I knew something was coming I just didn't know what.

"You're just saying you're sorry, you don't even know or care what you have actually done, you think saying sorry will fix it well it won't and stop bloody doing that, it isnae helping." She said moving the hand I had been rubbing her back with, which had decided on its own to start caressing her bum, I think that's what she meant when she said it isn't helping.

I laughed softly, I knew it was wrong but I couldn't help it "It's your fault for lying on your stomach and just presenting your bum for rubbing." I said slapping the bum in question for emphasis.

"If I had lay here on my back you would just have started on my boobs, it's impossible to talk to you without you groping me" she said but not with anger.

"Guilty as charged" I said reaching around her and squeezing a boob.

She sat up abruptly and slapped the back of my head "Stop it, this is serious and you're not just getting me to have sex so I will forget all about it, you do that to me all the time" she said folding her arms across her chest to forbid access.

"Okay, alright" I said putting my head on her thighs and looking up at her "Tell me what's really up then"

She grabbed both sides of my face with her hands and said sternly "Sit up and I will tell you, in fact get off the bed, get away from me and sit over there and I will tell you" she pointed at the kitchen chair that was in front of the chest of drawers beside the window, which was where I used to sit when doing my homework. I gave her my very best petulant spoiled wee boy look, but she was adamant, so reluctantly, I got up and sat where I was told to sit.

"You let your sisters and your Ma bully me" she said again folding her arms across her chest as if she was ready for a fight.

I gave in straight away "I don't mean to let them do anything, I didn't realise you seen it as bullying. I thought they were treating you the way Dot and Darlene treat each other, they shout and bawl a bit find a compromise or agree to disagree and get on with it, is that not what they have been doing with you?" I asked.

"No, not really" she replied "They sort of do something and then tell me that it's done instead of talking to me about it. I mean last week your Ma tells me your two aunties are putting on a buffet for the wedding. When I asked her what sort of stuff they were doing because I love vol au vents, she said 'well hen it's too late now for you to decide what's going to be in the buffet"

"That's just my Ma's way, she just gets on with things and gets them done, look at Christmas in this house it's a major production feeding and watering twenty odd people but my Ma just gets it done and nobody is any the wiser of when and how she did it, she just does it and that's it" I said trying to play the middleman.

"This isn't Christmas Danny, this is my wedding" she said.

"Our wedding, and Charlie and Iris's wedding" I said back at her.

"That doesn't stop it being my wedding Danny and now you are taking your Ma's side as well" she said, the arms which had dropped into her lap were back across her chest again.

"There isn't any sides here Patricia, my Ma's just being my Ma, but if you want to be more involved then you have to tell her, and not just moan at me about it." I said a wee bit harshly

She looked at me with a flash of vulnerability, "I canny tell her, you need to tell her, I'm too scared"

"Patricia in two week's time you're gonny be Mrs McCallister, do you really want me to fight your battles for you with my Ma, Dot and Darlene, and do you think that will work. You need to stand up to them yourself"

"I canny, I'm scared of them. Your Ma just looks at me as if I'm stupid and I start stammering and feel like greeting all the time. And if I argue with Darlene or Dot they will just batter me. I saw Darlene batter somebody in McCulloch street a couple of months ago, and I mean batter, she fights like a man, she just ran at this lassie and punched her straight in the face, and then started kicking her when she fell on the ground." She said wide eyed and gorgeous.

I laughed gently "She wouldn't do that to you, you're family, she would never lift her hands to you, nobody would, they know I would kill them' or worse than that, I would never talk to them again." I paused and said "You need to stand up for yourself hen, if I do it they will just keep treating you the way they are just now"

"I will stand up for myself Danny, just not yet." She said again with a vulnerability that brought a lump to my throat. I went over to her and kissed her and held her "Okay, I will sort it" I said.

I went through to the kitchen and tried to be diplomatic. "Darlene, just leave her alone you skinny cow" I said, which I thought was short sweet and to the point. After about five minutes we stopped screaming at each other and I agreed not to call her a cow and she had agreed not to be a cow, so that was that sorted.

"Ma, what's my Aunt Jessie's address, me and Patricia are gonny jump on the subway and go and see her about the buffet." I said ready for battle.

"It's too late, the buffet's decided" my Ma said not even looking up from the sewing she had in her hands.

"No it isnae, don't tell me they have bought the food yet, it's two weeks to go, anything they bought just now would be off by the day of the wedding. Are we not having fresh food then, is it all just frozen rubbish" I said belligerently.

Charlie said to me "Mind your mouth Danny boy, shout at Darlene as much as you want, but that's my Ma you are shouting at now" I looked at him and for the first time, in probably a year or more I got mentally prepared to fight him.

"Don't you two halfwits start now" my Ma said "Are you gonny jump every time she tells you Danny, look at you, falling out with everybody just because she got a wee bit weepy, she's sixteen, she's just a wean. You canny fall out with everybody every time she greets."

"Aye Ma, for your information I will be jumping every single time she tells me, and don't think I started this, you know what's going on here and it isnae me or Patricia that started anything" I said " I won't let any of you'se treat her any way you'se like, including you Ma"

She looked at me I think she was trying to see how far I was prepared to go, she had her answer it was in my eyes. "Forty two Cadogan street, and take your auntie Jessie a wee box of Black magic, she will do just about anything for a box of chocolates, in fact during the war it was a pair of nylons she would do anything for" and she had a wee laugh to herself and gave me a look that told me, I had won the battle but not the war.

As it turned out the box of chocolates did the trick. Patricia got on with my auntie Jessie like a house on fire and approved everything she was doing for the buffet and was actually full of praise about how good it was and how lucky we were to have her to organise it.

My aunt Jessie was all over Patricia telling her how beautiful she was and how lucky she was to be able to get makeup and stuff like that because when she had got married just after the war and all the lassie's had had to draw a line up the back of their legs with a heavy pencil to make it look like they had stockings on, but before drawing the line they had to rub in something that was called liquid stockings, it was like a make up for your legs and the more you rubbed in the darker your legs got. And when people like her couldn't afford liquid stockings they would try stuff like rubbing in used tea leaves or coffee grounds from the local café.

So Patricia was a bit happier, but I didn't think we had heard the last of this, and I wasn't wrong the same problem would rear its head a couple of years later and cause quite a bad situation. The following week seemed to be spent with Patricia dragging me between pillar and post looking at things that meant absolutely nothing to me.

We were getting married in Martha Street at the registry office there, then the reception was to be at the Masonic Halls on Butterbiggins road in Shawlands, just opposite the bus garage. We couldn't get the reception hall until five o'clock so there was to be a break of three or four hours between the weddings and the reception. My Ma decided that we should spend that time in her house at Cessnock Street, so Patricia and her decided between them that there should be a sort of mini buffet set out for whoever was coming to Cessnock, because the buffet at the reception wouldn't be opened until about nine.

Charlie, my Da and me were agreed, who cares if people are hungry they can get a mars bar or something out of Mr Patel's or if they are really hungry they can buy themselves a fish supper from the chippy, why should we have to feed them twice? Patricia and my Ma were united in thinking that we were ignorant peasants and had no idea what a wedding was supposed to be like. I had, over the last eight months, spent every single penny I had on this wedding. Admittedly that didn't amount to much, my Ma had asked me if I wanted a cash loan out of Fishers to help me out, but I said no we would make do with whatever we could afford.

Patricia's Ma was a single parent and had two or three jobs on the go just to keep the wolf from the door, so she couldn't contribute. My Ma and Da probably put a bit more money into than they told us, but I couldn't expect them to buy Patricia's outfit or pay for my hired suit or anything like that.

Another handy thing was that Donnie was to be my best man and Dunky was to be Charlie's best man. So Donnie paid for all the flowers, despite moaning the face off Patricia for picking the most expensive bouquet which had as many feathers in it as flowers, and he also paid for his own suit hire which I thought was very good of him at the time. Both Dunky and Donnie knew I was pink lint and they along with Tony and my Da, slipped some money to me on the day of the wedding to make sure I could buy drinks when I had to. I was very grateful that they did because I hadn't even thought about that and by the time the wedding came round I would probably have had about a tenner in my pocket if they hadn't done what they did.

I am sure Patricia would have loved a fairy tale wedding with a huge wedding dress and train, and loads of bridesmaids all dressed in chiffon and silk, and pageboys and flower girls scattering rose petals in her path. What she got was a budget wedding, she did wear a lovely white dress though, it was a below the knee dress with a sort of pleated skirt at the bottom and a crossover top with crystal pleats above, it was very like the dress Marilyn Monroe had on which got blown up around her by the wind in some movie, and then a white box jacket on top of that. Along of course with the white stilettos and handbag and all the trimmings we could afford. This included a blue garter we would have lots of fun with on the day. Her bridesmaid, her sister Betty, wore the same ensemble but in pale blue, but without the garter, as far as I knew. And again Betty had helped us out and paid for all of it herself, much to the disgust of her husband Tommy.

Charlie took it all in his stride his main concern and one of my Ma's main concerns was that Iris was well on in her pregnancy and nobody wanted the same situation we had with Annie at her and Donnie's wedding. Where she gave birth on her wedding day following what could only be described as a riot. And if memory serves me well theirs was a double wedding also in the masonic Halls at Butterbiggins road, the omen's weren't good.

"She will be here Danny, there's still half an hour to go" Donnie said to me, lighting me a fag and handing it to me. We were stood outside the registry office waiting for some sign of Patricia showing up, everybody else was here except her and her family. They were all coming together in a couple of taxi's which were supposed to have been booked the day before.

"She won't Donnie, she has been worrying about this for weeks, maybe this week has just been too much for her, I just know she's changed her mind, I can feel it." I said forlornly.

"Danny it's pouring with rain, come inside and we can look through the doors for her coming, come on get in you're getting soaked" Charlie said as he walked out of the double doors of the registry office and pulled me by the arm towards the dry sanctuary of the hallway. He was enjoying my discomfort, I could see it in his grin.

"Of course it's pouring with rain, it always rains on Glasgow Fair Friday" I said grabbing Donnie's arm and looking at his Timex. Twenty minutes to go. The arrangement was that Patricia and I would be getting married at eleven thirty straight after Iris and Charlie who were down for eleven o'clock. There was now ten minutes left for her to turn up if she wanted to be there when Iris and Charlie did the business.

Two black Hackney taxi's appeared at the bottom of Martha Street and my heart gave a little lurch, "Please god let it be her and I will promise to be good forever" I was thinking. Hallelujah it was her and her ragbag entourage, "That's one I owe you" I told the big man upstairs.

"Come on Danny, its bad luck for you to see her before the wedding" Darlene said grabbing me and pulling at me, I probably wasn't supposed to hear her say to Donnie, "and it would have been a lot worse luck for her if she hadn't turned up" I said nothing I was too relieved to even begin to start in on Darlene. "Don't be daft Darlene she will be sitting beside me watching Charlie get married, am I supposed to sit with my eyes shut" I said, but still allowed her to drag me upstairs

"Here" Donnie said handing me a hankie that had seen better days, there was a tear right along one side where it had worn away, a brown stain all over another side of it and there was a hard corner where it was obviously full of snot "Wipe your forehead you're sweating like a pig" he said to me pointing at my face.

I handed him his manky hankie back and said "Are you joking, that looks as if you just wiped your arse with it"

He looked at it and said "Oh so it does" and started to unpick the hard corner to see what was in there, now I had an idea where Paul got his grotty habits from.

"Here she is" I said glancing back at the entrance to the room we were in, I made do with wiping the sweat off my face with the sleeve of my suit jacket. It was hired; surely they expect it to come back a wee bit dirty. She was being escorted along by Tommy Curry her older sister Betty's husband. Who was probably the nearest thing Patricia had to a father, Betty was also beside her as her bridesmaid. She was wearing a big wide grin, obviously something had happened that not only held them up but had also highly amused her as well.

I found out later that one of the taxi's they had got was being driven by a Nigerian guy who was driving around looking for Arthur street instead of Martha street, and that Tommy thought the louder he shouted, the higher the possibility that the Nigerian guy would understand him, So at one point Tommy and the Nigerian taxi driver had been squaring up to each other all ready to start boxing. It was only the arrival of the other taxi driver and his intervention that stopped a brawl in the middle of George square.

As they all rushed into the wedding room, I looked at Patricia, she had on a little pink pillbox hat with a veil that barely covered her eyes, which I hadn't seen before it matched her bouquet of flowers and the pink flower in her jacket lapel. I wanted to grab her and kiss her and kiss her again and show her, and tell her, how much I loved her and how I would always love her, and how I would always worship the ground she walked on, she would never in my eyes be capable of doing wrong. I also wanted to tell her she had almost given me a heart attack by being so late.

But at the same time I also felt the urge to faint. My head went woozy, I started to sweat again, like Niagara Falls after a rainstorm. My knees wobbled, I could feel my heart beating not only in my chest but at the side of my head, as if the vein there was throbbing in time with my heart, maybe it was, I thought. That must be like my pulse I thought as I listened to its steady rhythm and started to fall into a little trance. Donnie came to the rescue by doing what any best man does well, he improvised and got a hold of my pinkie and bent it back until it almost broke. I managed, only just, to stifle my scream and look at Patricia and if she had seen tears in my eyes at that point they were genuine, genuine tears of pain that is.

I couldn't take my eyes of Patricia but the fear or the nervousness, or whatever it was, was still hitting me in waves. I must have looked like a drunken sailor on a heaving deck. Donnie told me later that he didn't notice that and those feelings must have just been inside me, he also told me that I was acting like a wee poof. Patricia squeezed in beside me, because we were late we were off to the right hand side, rather than directly behind Charlie and Iris.it had an advantage because we could see Iris's expressions as she took her vows.

As the registrar worked her way through the ceremony Charlie's voice got quieter and quieter, I could hardly believe it, he was more scared than me. Never in my life had I seen Charlie McCallister scared and we had already at that age been in many many scary situations. He was shitting himself, and I can honestly say I seen his knees buckle at least twice and both times Dunky had to push him in the back to keep him upright. This was the perfect way to calm me down, my nerves left me completely, I knew all I had to do was avoid being a pillock during my wedding and I would be able to slag Charlie forever over his fear. It was priceless.

Charlie faltered on Iris's middle name, another bonus for me as long as I could remember that Patricia's middle name was Eileen. They got through it at last, and the nerves hit me again, it was our turn. Everybody was milling about hugging Charlie and kissing Iris, she looked lovely and was clearly delighted. He looked happy and was clearly relieved it was over. Patricia was by my side and holding my hand, I kissed her.

"Hoy you, you aren't supposed to do that yet, wait until you are told you may kiss the bride, before you start cleaning each other's tonsils" Dorothy said, as she separated me from Patricia. Patricia Eileen Miller, I kept repeating it over and over determined to get it right.

"Ladies and gentlemen can everyone take their seats, we have another happy couple to make even happier" the registrar said, I suppose it was slightly different for her, not that many double weddings with over one hundred guests take place at Martha street I would guess. She got us through most if it word perfect, although Patricia was very giggly. It turned out that Charlie was making faces at her behind my back, trying to get her to laugh. And then my big moment came, the bit I had practiced so as not to repeat Charlie's mistake.

"I take thee Eileen Patricia Miller, I mean Patricia Eileen Miller to be my lawful wedded life" I said, and went red. I don't think anybody noticed. Patricia got it word perfect through her giggling and I got told to kiss the bride, so I did.

Two of Patricia's aunties, Sarah and Doris were on the steps of the registry office throwing handfuls of wet confetti at us, it was still pouring, so the confetti came at us in clumps. Patricia's young brother, Rob, was with them and I thought he was taking particular delight in throwing clumps of wet confetti at his sister, well he was fourteen I suppose.

Nobody had thought of any transport to get us from the registry office to my Ma's for the pre-reception reception. So Donnie came up with the best idea, it was only a short walk to Buchanan street subway station. So that's exactly what we did, all one hundred and odd of us walked to the subway station and got a ticket to Cessnock. It was a chubby black woman in the ticket booth and she laughed and laughed as we all trooped through, and crowded the platform. When the train did come it was already standing room only but we just piled on anyway. By the time it got to Cessnock we practically fell off when the train stopped. There was a solitary old man waiting for the train, and he looked half drunk, he just kept staring at us all getting off and rubbed his eyes as if he was seeing things.

I think we lost a few stragglers who went to the pub rather than come and spend four or five hours in my Ma's waiting for the Masonic halls to open and let us in. But there were still at least eighty or ninety people in my Ma's house, in fact probably more because some of my pals who were supposed to be only coming to the reception had seen us arrive on the subway and decided to join us. Under ordinary circumstances I might have told them to go away but it was a wedding, you don't tell people to go away when it's a wedding, that's just not done.

The living room was full, the kitchen was full and the hall was full of people in varying stages of drunkenness. My Da wasn't helping, in fact, he was actually loving it. He had recently turned the big press in the living room into a fully functioning bar. Not only that but he had bought a full keg of lager from the pub so was having great fun showing off to my uncles, playing mien host.

I kept getting split away from Patricia, every time I thought there was an opportunity to sneak through to my room for a "private chat" somebody else grabbed me or grabbed her and dragged us up to dance or into a corner to ask us how we liked being married, after all of two or three hours. Still, I liked it fine so far.

My Da's bar went down a treat with everybody except my Ma. Her idea had been that the immediate families of both couples would come back to her house for a cup of tea and a sandwich and a wee chat, giving them a chance to get to know one another. What had in fact transpired was that there was now over a hundred people in her house, mostly pissed and looking for a way to get to Butterbiggins road, which is a good two or three miles from Cessnock street. I wasn't pissed but I was certainly half way there, Charlie was hardly drinking at all, for probably the first time he put Iris's needs in front of his and concentrated on looking after her rather than getting pissed with me, or anybody else.

Patricia was also quite well on, her pal Sally and her sister Betty had decided to open the half bottles of vodka that they had in their handbags ready for the reception hall later on. Bearing in mind that one of the reason's they had been late in the morning was Sally introducing Patricia to the fine tradition of bucks fizz in the morning, which they made with white wine since we couldn't run to champagne. Their reasoning for opening their emergency half bottles being that it was a Friday and Haddows would be open and they could get another couple of half bottles on the way to the hall.

Darlene was quite drunk already, although by her standards that meant still sober, and arguing with her husband, a lot, she was giving him a really hard time. I went to speak to her and see what was up. I hadn't really spent much time talking to her that day, there was too much to do without getting trapped in a conversation with Darlene, which with the best of intentions could quite easily waste half a day of your life in the blink of an eye.

I approached her from her left side as she was engrossed in a conversation with one of Patricia's pals from McCulloch Street. The fact I approached her from the side was probably why I noticed her black eye.

"Sorry sweetheart, I need my big sister for something, I will bring her back in a minute honest" I said to the girl she was speaking to.

"What the hell is that" I said pointing at the black eye on Darlene's face.

"What?" she said, looking at me with anger as if I had done it.

I dragged her out of the living room and pushed her into my bedroom, I couldn't help thinking that's what I should have done with Patricia, instead of trying to sneak her into the bedroom.

"That fuckin black eye, that's what" I shouted at her. "You better have been fighting with one of the bridesmaid or Dorothy" I shouted again "Because if that was that tadger Lawson, I'm going to kick his rotten teeth down his throat"

She looked at me, she was the big sister and I was the wee brother she smiled sardonically and said "Don't be stupid Danny, he's twice the size of you and anyway I can handle him, this was just a stupid accident. We were arguing and I started throwing punches at him and he put his arms up to stop me and his hand hit my face. He didn't mean it, and anyway it was my own fault, you know what I am like I just start throwing my arms about like a maddie, maybe I gave myself the black eye" she looked at me defiantly, she wanted to tell me to mind my own business, but she knew I wouldn't.

"Okay Darlene, you're right, I would probably struggle to do him on my own, he is too big. But an iron bar on the back of his head will bring him down to my height or I could just tell Donnie and Dunky. Or how's about I get Charlie to help me, him and me would be plenty" I said through gritted teeth, I knew she was making excuses for him, I turned away ready to go and find him and sort him out, whatever she said.

"Danny don't please" she said holding my arm "This is my problem, I will sort it out. I'm not lying, we were just arguing, it's not like he just lamped me one, he didn't. I gave as good as I got. Don't tell Donnie or Charlie, they will kill him. It's honestly not a big deal, anyway it's not as if all them are snow white, there's been plenty of black eyes in this family, including my Ma's"

"You mean they aren't as white as snow Darlene, not snow white, that was the lassie that hung about with dwarfs. I canny just let it go Darlene, I canny, My Da and Donnie would kill me if I didn't tell them. You know they both want any excuse to put his lights out as it is." I pleaded with her.

"Och shut up Danny, you think everything's blue and white, what about all the times My da hit my Ma or Tony hit Dorothy, grow up Danny it won't be that long before Patricia annoys you and you lamp her one. Maybe she will look at some boy, or be unhappy because you look at a lassie or you come in late or come in drunk, you will do the same, hit out and then be sorry, or at least kid on you are sorry." I hesitated before saying anything else, thinking that there had already been a couple of times where I had pulled Patricia about roughly and frightened her, but hitting her was out of the question.

"Don't be stupid all your life Darlene, My Ma didn'y have to put up with my Da hitting her and neither do you, you'se just think you'se do." I said shaking my head with resignation. "Okay I won't say a word to anybody as long as you promise the next time he lifts his hands you tell me."

She looked at me maybe assessing how far she could push me "He never lifted his hands Danny, but if he ever does, I will tell you. Or the police will tell you when they come to tell you that I have stabbed him. You're right about one thing Danny, I am not my Ma. And I know you think I'm a daftie because I get my words mixed up sometimes, but don't make that mistake Danny, I'm anything but daft son" she said with a steely look in her eyes that I recognised, I saw it all the time, in Charlie's eyes and in the mirror.

"I know, but I'm not daft either, Darlene, and my eyes are wide open" was all I said.

Naturally since I had told her I wouldn't tell anybody the first thing I did was ask Charlie if he had noticed her black eye, and the first thing he did was threaten to kill John Lawson. I calmed him down and explained what Darlene had said and told him she deserved the chance to sort it out herself before we started to interfere. At first he refused but when I explained he wouldn't be happy if somebody tried to butt into his relationship with Iris, or that I would go mental if he or anybody else stuck their nose into my life. He agreed, as I had, to bide his time but made no promises as to what the outcome would be if it happened again.

My Da made a few phone calls and came up with two people with mini buses who lived reasonably locally, one in Cardonald and one in Pollok, they went back and forth between the masonic Halls and my Ma's house until everybody was where they should be, they also came to the reception because my Da invited them. My Ma eventually stopped him asking everybody he spoke to, but not until he had extended the hand of friendship to quite a few more strangers.

The hall was exactly the same as it had been seven or eight years earlier when Dot's wedding reception had been there. I stood looking round and remembering the big fight between Tony's family and my family and then Annie going into labour. What a day that had been, it had been brilliant, I hoped our wedding would be as memorable but hopefully without the fighting and the childbirth.

The tables were arranged as per usual for a wedding, a long one across the front of the stage where the deejay would set up after the speeches and things, and the rest in rows at ninety degrees to the main table. But since we weren't having a sit down meal just a buffet it seemed a bit silly to have the tables like that just for the speeches, so when we got there we rearranged them down both sides of the dance floor. The disco was set up early so that those who were giving speeches stood on the stage and used the deejay's mike.

Donnie mumbled a few dirty jokes which he tried to change a little to make it appear they were about me and Patricia.  Dunky used his best man's speech mainly to use the advantage of being on the stage to swivel his hips and look round the room for available women. Patricia's Ma made a little speech in the space where the father of the bride would normally speak. She mainly put on a posh voice and thanked everyone for coming, individually.

 I gave a speech again thanking everybody for coming but not individually, I also thanked everybody that needed to be thanked like my Ma and Da and Patricia's Ma and I remembered what my Ma had told me earlier in the week and complimented the bridesmaid on how nice she looked. I told her that if I hadn't met Patricia first, and if she hadn't had five children with Tommy, that I wouldn't say no, if she asked me. Neither Patricia nor Tommy thought that I was funny, but I am sure Betty had a twinkle in her eye

Speeches done and with the various children getting bored and restless the signal was given to the deejay to get the music started by playing the first song for the brides and grooms to dance to. Apparently my Ma had chosen the song, I knew nothing about it nor did Patricia. The deejay played, "This time the girl is going to stay" by Elvis. Patricia was livid as was Iris, that was a very strange song to choose, what was my Ma trying to say "How many girls hadn't decided to stay" Patricia asked me, and I am pretty sure Iris was asking Charlie something similar judging by the look on his face.

Apart from that the rest of the night went really well, at one point Paul was up on the dance floor by himself in his brand new Teddy Boy suit giving a great display of jiving to another Elvis song. Patricia's grandfather "Jock the Plum" which was his nickname from his days as a docker on the Clyde, joined Paul at one point and then almost everybody in the hall stood in a circle around them and cheered them on, it was fantastic and really got the party going.

There was a slight down side later on when Patricia asked me to intervene in a minor disagreement between her granny and her brother in law Tommy. Tommy was as drunk as it is possible to be without passing out. Mrs Donaldson, Patricia's granny, accused him of peeing on the floor under the table they were sitting at. Tommy denied this strenuously and blamed either spilled drinks or some of the many children wandering about as being the culprits. Unfortunately when he stood up to remonstrate with his wife Betty who had been informed of this incident, the stain on the front of his cream trousers which extended the length of his inside leg and was still dripping slightly at the turn up told more truth than he wanted anyone to know.

He was bundled into the toilet, but after refusing to go home and sleep it off, Patricia's pal wee Sally was despatched with instructions to get on a bus go home and get him another pair of trousers. When she arrived back fifteen minutes later clutching a pair of jeans, I was very surprised since the bus journey from the hall to Tommy's house took more than twenty minutes each way.

"Hoy Sally come here, where did you get them, you haven't been away down to Kinning Park and back that quickly. Did you just rip them off the first guy you could get into a close" I said as I saw her enter the hall with the jeans.

"Beat it you, go and bother your wife" Sally said to me but still laughing.

"I can't believe you Sally, have you left some guy wandering about Shawlands in his pants" I asked laughing and added "Or is he still even wearing pants, or have you got them in your clutch bag for Tommy"

"Stop getting yourself excited Danny, Patricia will sort you out later. And anyway, these weren't being worn when I got them. I just went snowdropping" She said, lifting a drink from the empty table beside her and downing it in one.

"What's that?" I asked "I've never heard of that"

She laughed and said "Sometimes Danny you're so innocent, it's no wonder Patricia loves you, you'se are exactly the same. Head in the skies thinking everybody is nice. Snowdropping is stealing peoples washing

103

from their clothes lines when they aren't looking, usually during the night, some dafties leave their washing out all night so they deserve to get it nicked"

"No they don't Sally, anyway why is it called Snowdropping" I asked intrigued.

"How should I know, what do you think I am, a dictionary or something" she said walking towards the gents to give Tommy his new trousers.

I just laughed, I never did find out why it was called Snowdropping, it just sounded like thieving to me. Tommy's whisky induced incontinence problem apart, the rest of the night went brilliantly. Near the end of the night I was carried shoulder high by all of my brothers and some of our friends, Charlie was then given the same treatment. I called a halt when Dunky and Tony grabbed Patricia and lifted her above their heads, revealing to everyone in the hall that her knickers matched her white and pink outfit perfectly. I had to stop them particularly as they were heading for Iris next.

A taxi was called to take Patricia and me home, there weren't many left in the hall by that time. There never are when Patricia goes out, she likes to squeeze every last drop out of a party, and she is always the last to leave. We had Patricia's mum's house to ourselves for the night, her and her son Rob were staying with her sister Sarah and her kids, Alan and Isobel.

Our wedding night wasn't very much like it is in the movies. I tried carrying her over the threshold of her Ma's house in my arms. That didn't work the stairway up to the attic was too narrow and I kept banging her head off the wall. I tried to give her a piggy back, first of all she objected vehemently to me calling it a piggy back because she wasn't a pig, and how could I say that on our wedding night.

Secondly her dress was too tight for her to open her legs wide enough to get on my back, so when I said to her 'you need to open your legs wider than that' she went into a fit of giggles at the thought of her Ma's neighbours hearing me say that to her on our wedding night. So I did the only thing possible, I threw her over my shoulder and carried her up the stairs, saying 'Me Tarzan, you Jane" all the way up the stairs.

That seemed a good idea at the time, but when I got to the top of the stairs and put her down, she immediately lunged into the bathroom. My shoulder bumping into her stomach all the way up the stairs had made the copious amounts of vol au vents she had consumed earlier on from the buffet, want to evacuate the premises so to speak. So the first hour of our wedding night was spent with me holding her hair out of the way, while she was sick in the toilet.

It seemed to me at the time that she couldn't possibly survive that amount of vomiting without suffering internal injuries. It was frightening, she claimed a dodgy prawn the next day, I told her there was evidence that a prawn washed down with about twenty vodka and cokes could potentially cause a person to be sick. She insisted it was a dodgy prawn and that she had only had a few drinks, aye right.

Most of the rest of the night was spent with me getting her glasses of water and then sitting staring at her all night, scared that she would be sick in her sleep and die. It didn't help that we were in her Ma's haunted house and every creak made me jump like a startled frog. At one point I was convinced somebody was standing in the corner of the room and peeing into a po, then I realised I had left the bathroom tap running. I debated with myself whether to leave it running until it got light outside, because one of the ghost stories that I had been told started in the bathroom. I reasoned that it was July so it would be light by half past four or thereabouts so I could wait until then to turn the tap off, there was no use taking unnecessary risks.

I eventually fell asleep with no episodes of haunting to report. Patricia slept as if she was in a coma but woke up full of the joys of spring and anxious to get on with our honeymoon. We couldn't actually afford a day out to Saltcoats or Ayr let alone a honeymoon. We had arranged to stay in her grannies house and look after it for two weeks while they were away down to Lincoln to have a holiday with their daughter Doris and her husband James. I had only met James briefly once before. It was in Patricia's grannies house James and Patricia's Granda, Jock, had been having a bit of a bevvy session and James had got his accordion out and played a few tunes it had been a great night. James looked as if he weighed about seven stone and so did the accordion, when he picked it up to play you could barely see him, but he was fantastic at it, the whole house was bouncing.

# Chapter twenty two, Glasgow honeymoon and shaky starts.

We were supposed to pick up the keys to her granny's that morning, we eventually got out of bed at three in the afternoon, and only because Patricia's Ma turned up, wanting her own house back. This was our first two weeks as a married couple, I left the house three times in that two weeks to get bread milk and tins of beans, we lived on tea, toast and beans and each other. We spent roughly twenty hours a day in bed only getting up to eat and go to the loo. We had visitors for the first two days, Patricia's sister betty and her pal Sally, they must have got the message because they never came back for the full fortnight, maybe we should have got out of bed to talk to them, when they visited that first two days.

A decision had to be made whether we would live at my Ma's for the two months we were waiting for our house to be ready or at Patricia's Ma's. It wasn't an easy decision, I wasn't bothered either way, My house would be easier because all I had to do was to turf Paul out of my room which he now considered to be his room as I had got married and left home. When I pointed out to him that I didn't have a house yet and until I did that room would remain mine, he offered to fight me for it he was twelve. I had to stop Charlie being an influence on him, the next thing would be him becoming a Celtic supporter as well, which he eventually did by the way, silly boy.

The downside of staying at my house was that Patricia was afraid of my Ma, well not so much afraid as having the feeling that she was being constantly judged and found wanting. I didn't recognise that description of my Ma and convinced Patricia to stay at mine and see how it went. We stayed two weeks.

"Why are you crying" I asked Patricia, I had just come home. I had been down at the co-op in Govan trying to get my old job back, but Mr Wilson had retired.  Or rather he had been offered retirement rather than prosecution, quite a few items had turned up missing at an unannounced stock take. I am sure some of those anomalies may not have been down to me. There was a new manager in place who had a very condescending attitude and one of those pinched lip faces that you would never tire of punching, so even when he said he would take my phone number and call me if anything came up, I told him not to bother.

"Your Ma had a go at me" she said sobbing again.

"What about?"

"About you not working"

"Why is she having a go at you about me not working?"

"She said it's my fault that you don't get out of your bed in the morning and that I should be making you get up at eight o'clock, she made me feel as if she was accusing me of forcing you to stay in bed every morning to have sex or something. Instead of getting up and getting out there and finding a job. And I think she sort of implied that she canny afford to keep us forever." Patricia looked at me warily, maybe expecting me to get angry at her for talking about my Ma.

I was getting angry but not at her, I was angry at my Ma for involving Patricia but I also knew that we were sort of taking advantage. I wasn't working and Patricia was only working in the bingo at nights, which was part of the problem, because we could only see each other during the day I wasn't really putting any effort in to getting a job, figuring that if had a job, I would barely see her at all. But Patricia's wages at the bingo were rubbish, so we could only afford to give my Ma a tenner a week dig money. Patricia ate like a sparrow on a diet but I ate like a hungry hippo. I am sure my Ma was implying to Patricia that she couldn't keep us forever, she had said as much to me directly.

"She looks at me funny as well Danny when I am cleaning up or cooking something, it's like she wants to criticise but is holding her tongue. I was doing a washing the other day, I had the twin tub all loaded up and put soap powder in and she came in and took half of the washing out and said 'That's two loads' and just walked away. I burst into tears and stood greeting into the washing, she hates me" Patricia said and started sobbing again.

"She doesn't hate you, don't be ridiculous, she's just helping you and you are taking it the wrong way." I said trying to console her.

"So you think I am stupid then? " She said turning on me "You think I canny tell when somebody doesn't like me is that it? You think I'm just a dumb blonde, don't you" She asked getting angrier and angrier.

I shouldn't have laughed "What has being blonde got to do with anything?" I said with a stupid grin.

"See, you're exactly the same, you think I'm stupid the same as your Ma does, in fact you think I'm just a pair of big boobs with long hair" she said getting really angry.

I knew I shouldn't be laughing, I honestly did, "Euuggh, why would I want a pair of big boobs with long hair, that sounds disgusting" I said attempting to cuddle her and maybe get a squeeze at those boobs, which was her fault for talking about them and drawing my attention to them, I was eighteen what did she expect.

"Get away from me" she shouted "I am trying to argue with you and you are just being a sex maniac, again" she moved out of my reach.

"It hardly makes me a sex maniac wanting to cuddle my wife" I said to her petulantly.

"But you are" she said "I don't think we have spoken to each other standing up since we got married"

"You say that as if it's a bad thing" I replied, sliding closer and taking my life in my hands by holding her.

"It's just not fair Danny, everybody picks on me and you think making love solves everything" she said working up to a petted lip.

"I know, it's an injustice" I replied.

We decided after two weeks of living at my house we would ask her Ma if we could live there until our house was ready, her Ma agreed but made it clear we would be feeding ourselves and would have to help her out when gas and electricity bills came in. We agreed even though we were still living off Patricia's meagre bingo wages. I had suggested to her that she should try and get double shifts, but considering I made the suggestion when she finished her shift on a Friday night at ten forty five and met me coming home from the pub, I think she was remarkably restrained in just saying no.

Being out of work hadn't restricted my nights out or my consumption of lager, on any given Friday night one or other of my brothers or even my Da would slip me twenty quid to make sure I could join them in one pub or another. Dunky and Charlie subsidised my Tuesday nights out where we played for the darts team in the Quaich bar. Every week I would tell them I wasn't going because I was skint and was sick of being a scrounger and every week they would tell me not to be stupid, the day before we moved out of my Ma's house Charlie had a word with me about money.

"No joy with any jobs yet Danny" Charlie asked me. I was sitting in the comfortable armchair in the kitchen reading a book, it was after nine o'clock on a Thursday night, almost time for me to walk down to the Capitol Bingo in Lorne Street and walk Patricia home.

"No Charlie, absolutely bugger all. Maybe I should have moved to Wales or something, anything's better than this, every day I am out there looking, yesterday I went into about forty places all along the Govan road, not one of them had anything going. It doesn't even have to be in engineering, labouring would be fine, sweeping the floors would be fine, I just need to bring some bloody money in, Patricia's getting sick of it. I think we might move in with her Ma tomorrow because Patricia thinks my Ma is sick of us living off her and my Da" I said, for some reason confiding in Charlie, which wasn't a normal habit of mine.

"And you with all them brains as well, what hope is there for all us stupid ones" he said laughing. "And my Ma won't be bothering she knows you kick in what you can, that's just your bird being over sensitive"

"My wife" I said, smiling.

"Oh that's right we married them didn't we, how did that happen, I don't know whether it was them that were pissed or us when that decision was made" he said and laughed. I didn't laugh with him, because I couldn't tell if he was being sarcastic and neither could I be bothered arguing with him if he was.

"Do you want to make some money" he asked looking shifty.

"No" I said, "No bad enough to go to jail for it anyway"

"You only go to jail when you get caught, and we're good we don't get caught." he said "Searcher has got a wee warehouse number lined up and we need a look out, are you up for it"

"What's up with Bobby the bear" I asked. Bobby would normally be their look out or on occasion their muscle.

"He's in the jail" he said grinning.
I laughed and said "You just said you'se don't go to jail because you'se don't get caught."

He laughed back and said "Did you not hear about Bobby getting the jail? Aw Danny it was brilliant. I wasn't there I only heard about it from Searcher. Bobby and Searcher had checked out this wee cleaners shop, Searcher noticed the guy that owned the shop going to the bank on a Friday at dinner time and followed him in and stood behind him in the queue. The guy handed over one of them wee leather bank bags and the guy in the bank said there was just over a thousand pounds to go into his account. So the following week searcher waits outside the cleaners and follows the guy to the bank again, same thing, this time just under a thousand quid"

"So they robbed him the next week and Bobby got caught" I said taking a short cut to the inevitable end of his story.

"No, no. listen" Searcher decides robbing this guy is too dangerous because it would have to be in the middle of Paisley road in the middle of a Friday afternoon, when the place would be hoaching with people, so he decided that they will break into the guys shop from the back on the Thursday night and just grab the cash, even if it's in a safe they can just take that and open it later." He stopped to have a laugh and then got on with the story without telling me what was funny.

"So that's it, they go down Walmer Crescent the very next Thursday and break in through the back wall, they have got the usual hammers and bolster chisels covered with cloth to keep them quiet, they spend about three hours making a hole in the wall that they can fit through. Searcher is through it like a greased rat up a pipe, it's a bit tight for Bobby, but you know yourself he's a fat bastard. So in they go and would you believe it the guy hasn't got a safe, he just keeps the money in the till. Searcher said they got over six hundred quid which probably means they got near a grand" he says and grins again.

"But if they got away with a grand how come Bobby is in the jail" I ask.

"Right, Searcher is in the office looking for a safe and canny find one, eventually he thinks of looking in the till and finds the dosh, he grabs it and shouts at Bobby that it's time to go. Bobby is filling plastic bags with clothes off the rails in the back shop. Searcher tells him to dump them they have got a pile of cash and he wants out of there. Searcher is out of the hole in the back wall and bolting down to Cessnock Street quicker than a Cheetah's sneeze, but when he gets there he realises no Bobby. So cursing and swearing back he goes. He gets to the hole they made and there's Bobby half way through but stuck. Searcher grabs his arms and starts pulling him but he canny move the stupid fat bastard, he's too heavy"

"So he thinks it might be easier to push him back in and make the hole a bit bigger if they can. So he starts putting his feet on Bobby's shoulders and pushing him back in. Bobby starts shouting at him that it's too sore. Searcher stops and looks at Bobby and realises why he is stuck, he has got about five layers of clothes on. When searcher starts shouting and bawling about it, Bobby explains that rather than stick all the clothes he fancied in a bag he thought it was easier to put them on, because that would leave his hands free in case he needed them"

"Searcher started kicking him and screaming at him, he said he was trying to force him into the hole so he could strip off the clothes, but I think he was just trying to kick some sense into him. Anyway the next minute a window gets thrown open behind them and a woman starts shouting that she can see what they are up to and that she has phoned the polis, and right enough just as she says it, they can hear a siren. Searcher gets frantic, he knows he's got a right nice bundle of money in his sky rocket but he canny just leave the fat eejit can he." Charlie pauses probably just to build the suspense, he tells a good story.

111

"Searcher's got no choice he has to just leave him, it's Bobby's own stupid fault, so he tells him that he will probably get a fine but it's alright he will cover it and says see you later big man and bolts. He comes back about half an hour later but and joins the crowd that are watching the fire brigade knock a bigger hole in the wall so they can get Bobby out, and when they do he has about four brand new looking suits on, one on top of the other and he's shouting at the polis that they belong to him, even though the suits have all got dry cleaning labels on them"

Charlie has a good laugh at his own story, before asking me again "So that's why we need an edgy on this wee warehouse job tomorrow night"

"No" I said immediately "I would rather be skint than in the jail"

He looked at me as if I was the stupidest person on earth and shrugged his shoulders "So what will you do for money then? Have you signed on at the broo at least?" he asked.

"No, do I look like a beggar to you?" I asked him in return.

"Aye, actually you do" he said shaking his head and walking away.

He was right it had been a few weeks now if I couldn't find something rapid I would need to sign on, it was something I had never done and I really didn't want to, but Charlie had told me that if I did then the broo would have to pay my rent because there was no way Patricia's wages were going to. When we had signed the missive for the house we had both been working that's why we got it. So I decided if I didn't find a job this week then I was going to sign on.

Me and Patricia were sitting in my room trying to decide whether we were definitely going to move to her Ma's or whether we should just stick at out here for the couple of months we needed to wait for our own house. My Ma shouted on me that Charlie was on the phone, he needed me it was urgent apparently. I went on the phone and before he could say a word I gave him a mouthful of abuse and told him I wasn't interested in thieving with him and Searcher. He got a word in edgewise eventually and told me iris was in labour and that he was in the waiting room of the maternity ward of Rottenrow hospital. I put the phone down and ran without even saying anything. I was there in twenty minutes.

"Has she had it yet?" I asked, breathlessly approaching him and instinctively hugging him. I had a huge grin on my face he looked like he had seen a ghost.

He shook his head and then grinned as hugely as I had "I'm petrified" he said. I laughed and said "Don't be stupid, women have weans all the time, look at my Ma she's had nine and Annie look at her, she's had five rapid" he didn't look any less worried.

"I know that Danny, I'm sure she will be ok, that's no what I am worried about" he said and then paused for dramatic effect and then dropped his big joke "What if it's black" he finished and immediately started laughing his head off.

I don't know why I was even surprised, he was an idiot at the best of times why should I be shocked at his stupidity now. When he settled down he told me how Iris had been in labour for about four hours before telling him and he had now been here for almost three hours so she had been in labour for seven hours altogether. When we asked an older guy in his forties if seven hours in labour was a long time, he said he wasn't sure but he had been in a trade union for twenty one years and it hadn't done him any harm.

It took all of my strength to hold Charlie back from throttling him, he kept shouting at him "Its gonny do you harm now you champer"

We played I spy, we played poker dice, Charlie had a set in his pocket. We played pitch and toss, we tried to play twenty questions but Charlie still couldn't master what animal vegetable or minerals meant. Seven hours turned into ten hours which turned agonisingly slowly into fourteen hours.

A nurse came casually in and announced he was wanted in the delivery room, the baby was nearly here. He was stuck to the seat.

"You go Danny" you're better at this sort of thing. Both the nurse and I burst out laughing.

113

"You go to this one Charlie, and I will go to the next one I promise" I said when I got control of myself. The nurse eventually took his arm and said "Come on Mr McCallister, it's not sore, well not for you anyway"

He was only away for fifteen minutes before he came back into the waiting room.

"It's a wee Charlie, Danny. I mean it's a wee boy, and we're calling him Charlie, and he's beautiful Danny, really beautiful" he said and then he cried. He sobbed. It was obviously tears of joy and relief, he had been wound so tight over the last few hours it had to come out somehow.

I cuddled him laughing and joking with him that he was supposed to be a hard man from Govan and what would people think if they could see him now. I told him if I had a camera I could blackmail him forever. Eventually I asked how Iris was and at first the question threw him for a second but then he recovered and said "Aye, she's alright, I think, I will ask a nurse"

She was perfectly alright and if anything when I saw her she was even happier than Charlie and he was happier than a dog with two tails. I sat in the waiting room in a mood of euphoria, I had never seen Charlie so happy and I hoped it would get him to screw his head on and grow up.

The police arrived at three in the morning to let Patricia know that I had been arrested for drunk and disorderly conduct along with my brother Charles McCallister and that I would be appearing at the Sheriff court at eleven o'clock the next morning. We could probably start growing up some other day.

I got a twenty pound fine which I was supposed to pay at one pound per week from my giro, but Charlie paid it on the spot while he was paying his own. He asked me why we had been arrested, I asked him the same question, neither of us had an answer. We later found out that Charlie had been nakedly dancing in the rain outside Fergie's bar at the paisley road toll, and that I was fighting with two men who were remonstrating with him and telling him to put his clothes on. Apparently I told them that their ugly wee wives who were with them would eventually get over seeing a man size willie and accept what they had was all they were going to get. I suppose that explained my black eye.

Patricia was fine with it eventually, she didn't quite get how Charlie got naked, maybe she didn't quite understand Charlie yet. My Ma wasn't very chuffed with all the palaver either and it further increased the tension between her and me, so I agreed with Patricia let's try staying with her Ma for the few weeks left before we got our own house.

We moved all of our belongings out of my Ma's and up to Patricia's Ma's house in one day, in fact it took two suitcases and a black bin bag and that was it. Patricia got a loan of one her wee niece's prams and we walked the whole lot up Shields road in the rain. I wasn't happy about it, I thought we were jumping from the frying pan into the fire. At least at my Ma's there was always food in the fridge, okay she liked a wee moan now and again but so what? It wasn't the end of the world.

Her Ma gave us our own room which actually meant moving a single bed into the living room for Rob, Patricia's wee brother. He was a fourteen year old annoyance at the best of times, but he was being really obnoxious now, I suppose turfing him out of his own room wasn't that great for him either.

"Why do I have to sleep in the living room, how can they not do it?" he was wailing at his Ma and actually throwing a near tantrum.

"He needs his arse skelped and told to act his age" I whispered to Patricia, who elbowed me and mouthed "Shut up" Which I suppose was fair enough, but it reinforced my feelings that we were making a mistake.

"Here this is for your room Patricia" her Ma said, handing her an alarm clock pre-set for seven o'clock. I caught on right away Patricia didn't. Patricia worked nights so the clock was obviously set as a dig at me, implying she wanted me up at seven and out looking for work I suppose.

"There's no need to be funny Mrs Miller I would be getting up early and out looking for work you know. You didn't have to set the clock for me" I said with an undertone of anger in my voice.

She looked at me with derision "Well if you are getting up early that wee clock should help, it's been getting me up at seven, for my work, for long enough"

I didn't even have the guts to apologise, I just walked out of the living room and went into the tiny room that was to be our bedroom for the next six weeks. I did go looking for work every day for the next couple of weeks. I trudged round a few industrial estates and even contacted a couple of employment agencies, but it was the beginning of the Thatcher era in Scotland and jobs were scarce. The only ray of sunlight I got was a Saturday shift in the bookies at the end of McCulloch Street. It happened by chance because their usual board marker didn't turn up one day and I offered to have a go.

On the surface it seemed easy, the marker got a bundle of sheets of paper about the size of a newspaper but all that was marked on them was the names and numbers of horses or dogs in a specific race. These would be attached to a large white board that ran the length of the bookies shop. My job was to write the odds for each horse beside its name and then alter it when changes of odds were announced. It all looked and sounded simple but on a Saturday there are twenty four dog races and at least fifty six horse races. So keeping track of all the races and all the odds for every dog and every horse was difficult to say the least.

Add into the mix that all of my information came over 'the blower' which was a closed circuit radios system that was broadcast to all the bookies shops. The problem was that it was difficult to hear and keep up with the constant changes of odds made even more so by the babble and chatter of almost forty men and a few women.

Getting the odds right was critical if I missed an increase in the odds then punters would scream abuse at me because they may have lost out on some winnings. One punter threatened to stab me once because I missed a change in odds from three to one, out to four to one and he had placed his bet at the lower price of three to one. Both the manager of the shop and I manhandled him out of the shop and threatened him with the police if he came back. The manager let me know later that my mistake had cost the guy the princely sum of fifty pence. On the occasions where I missed a decrease in the odds it was the manager who was on my back, although to be fair he never once threatened to stab me.

The bookies shop itself was typical of most bookies shops, it was slightly grimy and slightly seedy and attracted during the week mostly a mix of the unemployed, the unemployable, pensioners of both sexes and the addicted gambler. Saturdays were different because most working guys like to put a football coupon on and put a couple of quid on the horses while they do. The Saturday crowd were looked on as amateurs by the midweek crowd, who all thought that they could be professional gamblers if only they could raise a large enough stake. When I pointed out to them that coming in with two quid and losing it all was exactly the same as coming in with two thousand quid and losing all of that they disagreed ferociously.

Apparently they would gamble 'differently' if they were betting more money, the vague explanation for this was that they wouldn't take as many risks and would only bet on sure things. When I pointed out that if they used their two quid and only bet on 'sure things' then there two quid would increase rapidly to a point where they had a big stake. They told me unanimously that I didn't understand anything about gambling at all and should get out of the bookmaking industry and go back to being an engineer. I agreed.

Although there were a few times when things did go well for them and even very occasionally for me. There was an old woman, Mrs Parsons was her name she lived up the next close to Patricia's Ma, she came in very day and put a twenty pence bet on a list of ten or twelve horses, never less than ten and never more than twelve. I was told that she had been doing this for at least four years and had never won a penny. Whenever I was in the bookies whether I was working or not, she would come over and ask what I thought of her selections and every single time I would tell her I was sure that this was the day she would come good.

And one day she did and thankfully for me it was a Saturday and I was working. She came in early as she always does and it was only the dogs that were on. The dog racing started at ten am until twelve am and then the horses would start. She came in and spotted me and as usual asked me to have a look at her line and give my opinion. I told her I wanted a good look and that she should get us both a cup of tea while I checked her selections over. She had chosen thirteen horses, I didn't know whether to point this out to her or not. All the what if's ran through my head, what if I didn't mention it and the thirteenth horse lost, what if I did mention it and she scored off a horse that could have won her some money.

Eventually I decided that I should tell her just in case she was superstitious.

"Mrs P. You have picked thirteen horses did you know that you had done that?" I asked her as she returned with my tea and a wee cup for herself. When I was marking the board I was on a sort of narrow stage that ran the length of the board. You got on to it by climbing three steps at the far end.

Mrs P sat on the top step and sipped her tea and answered me "I didn't count them Danny, they all just jumped out at me this morning, but if it is thirteen I will score one out. What one do you think has the least chance of winning?" she asked perusing the list of names in her hand.

I came along to her and lifted her list to have another look and couldn't believe the name of the last name on her list was unlucky for some in the five thirty at Pontefract. It was a bumper race for untried horses which basically meant that anything could win it, it was no better than a lottery.

"I would leave them all on Mrs P" I said "After all maybe it is a good omen" After a quick look at her list there were at least five other horses that would need individual miracle to let them win.

"Aye maybe it is Danny, maybe thirteen is just 'unlucky for some' I'll leave it as it is and cross my fingers" She said sipping away at her milk-less tea and smiling. It was a Saturday so the shop filled quickly and the blower started chattering at full speed and my concentration was completely on making as few mistakes as possible so naturally I forgot about Mrs P's line.

Until five o'clock when John Bell the owner of the bookies and the manager shouted over to me "Have you been watching out for Mrs P's horses" I presume he only asked because I had told him and another couple of the regulars about how unusual it was for her to pick thirteen horses and the last one to be called unlucky for some. I shook my head and he held up both hands fingers splayed out wide. "Ten winners?" I asked "How many losers?" He held up his thumb and forefinger circled indicating zero, I burst out laughing he shook his head. About fifteen minutes and a couple of results later he came out from behind the counter and approached me.

"Danny, that's twelve winners, she's just waiting for 'unlucky for some' in the last race at Pontefract." He said looking a bit shocked.

"Jesus Christ" I said "Oh shit, how much has she got going on?" I said part gleeful and part terrified.
"Over eight hundred quid" John said, with a huge grin.

  The odds were on the board for 'unlucky for some' it was eight to one, that meant if it won then Mrs P would win over seven thousand pounds. But if it lost she won nothing. That's why I was Terrified, I had persuaded her to leave the last horse on her accumulator if she hadn't she would be collecting over eight hundred quid right now which was an absolute fortune for her, her pension was probably about twenty five quid a week at most.

"Have you laid any of it off" I asked John.

He shook his head grinning like a loony. Normally when a bookie is exposed to a potential loss of that size he will 'lay it off' which basically means he will spread the bet with other bookmakers so that he minimises his losses. For example in this case he could bet a thousand pounds on 'unlucky for some' with another bookmaker and if it won, he would collect nine thousand pounds, pay Mrs P her winnings and still be quid's in. And if it lost he would only be down one thousand pounds instead of seven.

"Are you going to lay it off" I asked, totally surprised that he hadn't already.

"No" he said with a huge grin "I fancy a bit of excitement"

I burst out laughing and said "Don't be crazy, if that horse wins you're down seven grand and if it loses you have only won twenty pence, because that's all Mrs P put on her accumulator. That's mental" I said also now grinning.

It was five minutes to the race time, and John was starting to sweat he came out from behind his counter and approached me again.

"Well did you lay it off" I asked, he shook his head. "For fuck sake" was all I could think to say.

The race started and we listened to the live commentary, both of us totally absorbed. For whatever strange reason we both stood staring at the speaker up in the corner of the shop where the live commentary was coming from as if it was a television. There were only about a dozen customers in, the last race was at five forty five so all but the hardiest and most desperate gamblers were still there.

Throughout the commentary of that race my heart was beating at twice its normal rate, sweat was pouring down my face and I had never been so exhilarated in my entire life. I understood completely what drove those gamblers to cast everything they owned on the roll of a dice or the toss of a coin. And I wasn't even directly involved, I stood to lose or again, precisely nothing. John Bell was naturally even more excited than I was, he was enthralled by every word. His fists were opening and closing, with every piece of commentary. Every time the commentator mentioned 'unlucky for some' he would say "Fall you bastard" and every time the commentator would mention 'Auntie Dot', the favourite in the race he would shout "Come on you sack of shit, run faster"

It was all over bar the shouting, 'Auntie Dot' was twelve lengths clear at the last fence, 'unlucky for some' was back in third place, John Bell was beaming like a lighthouse and he punched me lightly on the arm. "See wee man, could you feel the buzz. That's why I don't gamble because that buzz can rot your soul" he said moving towards his desk behind the counter no doubt ready to count his winnings for the day. I hope Mrs P's twenty pence would stick in his throat.

"Good golly, Auntie Dot the seven to four favourite has fallen at the last hurdle, how extraordinary" the race commentator announced.

John froze in mid stride and turned and stared at the speaker on the wall as I did and we both heard the commentator describe how 'unlucky for some' overtook 'the wee rascal' to win by half a length. I was stunned, utterly and completely stunned. John Bell had a frozen grin on his face that looked like rigor mortis had set in, he was as white as a sheet. Eventually after a moment or two of silence I burst out laughing, I was laughing so hard I dropped to my knees. And to John's eternal credit, he joined me. The rest of the punters couldn't understand why the manager and the boardman were virtually rolling about on the floor laughing.

When we had both recovered I finished up marking the odds for the last race and when it was over I locked the doors and busied myself taking down all the racing newspapers around the walls and tidying up my area. I could see him with a pencil and pad in front of him settling bets and putting some in the winner's box and some in the losers.

I approached the window "How much" I asked quietly.

"Seven thousand four hundred and forty three pounds and twenty eight pence" he said, his head hanging down. "That's about two months profit for me Danny"

"Oh well" I said "You might have to wait until next year to replace the jag" and I laughed out loud.

So did John to be fair, but he looked at me and said not unkindly "One of these times wee man, you will make a joke at the wrong person, your mouth is quick, but I hope your feet are quicker."

Mrs Paterson wouldn't know about her win until Sunday morning, she never checked her bets until she got her newspaper of choice The Sunday Post delivered in the morning, I volunteered to go and give her the good news. John gave me four hundred pounds and asked me tell her she could collect the rest of her winnings on Monday, if she would come in first thing he would arrange either a cheque or cash whatever suited her.

She was overwhelmed when I told her, in fact she almost fainted. I had to get her a glass of water and then make her a cup of tea. She just couldn't comprehend the amount of money involved. At first she said to me she would take it in cash, she would stick some of it in her wardrobe and the rest in her purse. I explained to her that she couldn't do that, there were people living in this street or in any street that would choke their Granny for a fiver never mind thousands of pounds. She agreed with me that on Monday she would collect a cheque from John and I would go to the post office with her and help her set up a savings account.

As I left she tried to force me to take some money for 'all my trouble' as she described it, I refused, telling her that listening to her last horse win was probably the most exciting thing I had ever experienced. She collected her money and opened the account on the Monday as we planned, on the Tuesday she put an envelope with a hundred pounds through Patricia's Ma's door with my name on it and a wee note saying that if I didn't keep it she would never speak to me again. I kept it of course and it came in very handy indeed. Mrs P never again put a bet on to my knowledge. I met her in Harry Singh's the grocery shop next door to the bookies one day and asked her why she didn't bet again, she told me that something like that could never happen again so why bother. She was probably in her mid-seventies at the time. When she died about ten years later she left her only son, who lived in Essex and very rarely came back, over seven thousand pounds in her will. She basically hadn't spent a single penny of her winnings.

## Chapter twenty three; home sweet home.

We had the keys and we were ready to move in to our marital home, our landlords 'The West of Scotland Housing Association' gave us the keys at the end of September 1980 with a move in date of first of October. Patricia was very excited that she could now decorate the house and furnish it to suit us. The excitement didn't last long when I told her we had about fourteen quid to spare after we paid the rent and the two months deposit the landlord demanded. Bearing in mind that the fourteen quid might also be needed to pay bills and feed us.

"Should we not bother with having a house and just stay with my Ma for a while until we can save up money for some furniture and that." Patricia asked me glumly.

We were sitting on the floor of our new living room facing the windows that looked out on to McCulloch Street. We were contemplating the enormous task in front of us, of how to furnish and decorate a room and kitchen, hall and bathroom, with basically no money. I told her that's the advantage of having a big family everyone would rally round. And we did have some stuff, we had wedding and engagement presents unopened. There was a nice blanket, a sixteen piece dinner set, with plates, side plates, cups and saucers, in a nice earthenware brown with flowers on it. As well a set of pots and pans and a cutlery set. And some wee knick knacks, like ornaments and things.

"Including", I told her, "Two wee dolls with knitted dresses on to cover the toilet rolls that her Granny had personally knitted for us."

She laughed and said "Do you think my Granny could knit us a cooker and a washing machine"

Which got us both laughing and rolling about on the floor, she stopped me before I could talk her into consummating our relationship with the new house on the living room floor by screeching that there was no curtains or netting on the windows, just as I got her bra off. She was unimpressed when I suggested we used the big cupboard in the hall, unimpressed but still willing to give it a go.

Darlene still lived in the same street and I suggested to Patricia that we go up and see her and find out if she had anything she could spare us, maybe some curtains or netting or something, anything really.

When we got to her door it was partly open, not wide open but a gentle push opened it completely. When I did open it I could hear a baby crying, Darlene's son John was almost four and her daughter Charlene would have been about eighteen or twenty months, it was her I could hear crying. Patricia and I entered the house, it was dark and dismal in the hall, I tried to put the light on but it wasn't working. I presumed it was just a bulb that had conked out, because I could see a light from the living room. When we into the living room there was a single standard lamp lit up.

Wee John was sitting at a kitchen table which was in the living room playing with a couple of toy cars, wee Charlene was standing up in a filthy mesh playpen bawling her eyes out. Wee john spotted us and ran over to be lifted shouting "It's uncle Danny" I picked him up and gave him a cuddle and said to Patricia "Gonny lift the wean and see what's up with her, see if you can settle her down" And then I put John back down in the seat at the table and asked him where his Ma and Da were. He told me his Da was at work and his Ma was tired. It was nine o'clock at night, as far as I knew Big John worked during the day, but I did remember somebody saying he had got a job in a pub as a bouncer or something so it was possible that he was working, but where was Darlene? I checked the toilet first as I passed it on the way to the bedrooms, she wasn't in the toilet, there was plenty of dirty washing in there, on the floor and in the bathtub but no Darlene.

I checked the first bedroom I came to, which was clearly the kids' room, she wasn't there. Again plenty of dirty washing and even some dirty dishes on the floor and on every available surface but no Darlene, and no lights, it was also freezing cold. It was only October but it was Glasgow in October, it was freezing. I checked the last bedroom and at first I thought she wasn't there either. All I could make out were more bundles of dirty washing on the floor and on the bed and many more dirty plates and empty Irn Bru bottles strewn about the floor, as well as more than a few vodka bottles.

The bundle of dirty washing on the bed moved, my first thought was that it might be a rat, but if it was it was talking in Darlene's voice.

"Who's that, is that you John" she slurred.

I bellowed at her "No it isn't john, it's the social come to take your weans into care, you manky lazy bastard" Patricia came into the bedroom behind me and said "Shut up Danny you are frightening the wean" Wee Charlene was still sobbing but at least Patricia had her in her arms and was consoling her a bit.

I looked at them both and said "You need to get a nappy on that wean, it's freezing in here" She was half wrapped in a cover of some sort it looked like a bath towel rather than a baby blanket, but I could see that Charlene didn't have a nappy or pyjama's or anything on.

I looked at Patricia and shook my head, then turned to Darlene and asked her a question, she gave a muffled response from under the quilt that was over her, which I promptly pulled off her and kicked her on the side in an attempt to rouse her.

"Why is this house freezing, why are none of the lights working, who is supposed to be looking after your weans and where is that useless streak of pish you call a husband" I screamed at her punctuating each question by pushing her from side to side on the bed.

"leave me alone and go away" she said as she lifted the quilt back over her, I was about to grab the quilt and basically attack her, when Darlene grabbed me and told me to stop it the weans were watching and getting more and more upset and anyway Darlene was clearly steaming and incapable of answering anything.. She was right, wee John had a huge petted lip and snotters running out of his nose and into his mouth, Charlene was bawling again and her nose was also running like a tap.

"Right come on then wee man" I said, lifting John up and wiping his nose with a dirty dishtowel that was lying on the corner of Darlene's bed. Let's get your jacket on and we can go and visit your Auntie Patricia's mammy" We walked along McCulloch street with one wean each and Patricia looked visibly upset, and incredibly it was with me.

We got to her ma's house and her Ma was probably just as angry as me at the state of the weans
As I was, she made them a plate of tinned soup and some toast to dip in it. Patricia had grabbed a few of the weans' clothes and thrown them in a bag, we managed to get them reasonably dressed with dry clothes even if they weren't that clean. But there were no nappies for Charlene, Patricia used one of her Ma's hand towels as a nappy in the meantime. Her Ma agreed to watch the two weans so that Patricia and me could go back along and find out what was going on, Darlene could be self-centred and irresponsible at times but this was completely out of order.

I tried to wake her up but she was still way too drunk to answer questions with any sense, not that she had that much sense when she was sober. Patricia did her best to tidy the place up a bit, but it would have taken a team of cleaners a full weekend to make any inroads into the midden Darlene was calling a house. I discovered why there was no heat and only a lamp working in the living room. The electricity was cut off and the lamp worked by batteries. I was raging, I was kicking things about the room and shouting and bawling at Darlene despite the fact that she couldn't understand a word I was saying.

Patricia started crying and shouting at me. "Leave her alone, wait until she wakes up, maybe there's a reason it's like this and all you can do is shout and bawl. Stop shouting at her Danny I mean it. Leave her alone" So now Patricia was angry at me, what was I supposed to have done this didn't make sense at all.

"Okay okay, what's up with you" I asked "I have got a right to be angry at her, look at this midden and her weans are sitting her freezing and starving while she's lying in her bed as drunk as a skunk"

She wasn't crying now but she was still angry "How do you know what's happening, where's big John, how is he no here looking after the weans and how is it no his fault there's no electric and why is it only Darlene's fault that the place is filthy, is it no his fault as well?" she asked getting into her stride.

"I don't give a monkey's fart where he is, this is her house and her weans. I don't care if he's drunk dying or dead. She is a McCallister and this isn't on, and I'm gonny tell her that right after I throw a bucket of cold water over her head" I shouted back at Patricia.

"So, is that me told then, Mr big man, is that how you will treat me if I'm struggling. You're a McCallister get on with it and don't dare find it hard. You'se aren't as special as you think all the time Danny. Even McCallister's can find things hard sometimes and no cope." She said calming down and continuing to tidy as much of the mess as she could.

Determined to have the last word I said "That's where you are wrong sweetheart that's the one thing the McCallister's are good at is coping, it's a family speciality" I smiled but she didn't really smile back.

I popped back to her Ma's who agreed the weans could stay there that night, she would take them in beside her, so that I could try and find out what was going on with Darlene. At about three in the morning while Patricia and me were still tidying up, I must have taken about half a ton of rubbish down to the bins and there must have been a fivers worthy of ginger bottles all lined up in the hall, Darlene woke up and came into the kitchen which we had lit with a few candles we found in a drawer.

"What are you'se two doing here" she asked running her hands through her hair and coughing. She sat at the table beside us and took one of Patricia's cigarettes lit it up and asked me to make her a cup of tea.

"Is black tea with no sugar alright Darlene, because right now in your cupboard you have two teabags and a half a packet of rice, and the only thing in your fridge is a smell of sour milk" I said sarcastically, which wasn't true because I had went to the chippy at half ten and got some milk and sugar because Patricia struggles to go without tea for more than an hour.

I made her some tea and watched her drink it like an invalid sipping at it and chain smoking and rubbing her hair or her temples as if her head was louping.

"How are the weans?" I asked and she turned to look behind her as if they would be there. "Or more to the point, where are the weans?" I said almost but not quite shouting.

"Are you gonny start again Danny?" Patricia asked and said to Darlene "The weans are fine they are along in my Ma's, she will keep them until the morning, she's fine about it" Darlene looked annoyed at finding out we had taken the weans.

"We had to take them along there, the two of them were freezing and starving, Charlene had shite half way up her back and her arse is covered in a terrible nappy rash by the way, if you are at all interested. And wee John could make a rope ladder with the amount of hard snotters stuck to his face, it's lucky for you it was us that came in the night rather than the social, your weans would be in a home by now if it wisnae us that found them" I said starting to get angry and raising my voice.

Darlene got on her high horse "So your maw's fine about it is she, and what if I'm not fine about you taking my weans out of my house while I'm sleeping. They're my weans what's it got to do with you two what my weans are like. What if I'm not fine with a stupid wee lassie who used to be my babysitter and a stupid wee boy who thinks he's Alfred Frankenstein telling me what I can and canny do?"

Patricia looked at me shocked, I said "She means Albert Einstein" But I don't think that's what Patricia was shocked about, like me she was surprised that Darlene seemed oblivious to how badly she had let her weans down.

"Listen to me you half-wit," I started shouting again "Your weans were starving, they were probably about to start eating their own toes when we found them. You don't deserve to have weans somebody should take them off you" Then all of a sudden Patricia was shouting at me.

"What did I tell you Danny, leave her alone. Stop shouting at her why do you always think shouting makes things better. She's obviously struggling with something, her weans aren't normally this bad I used to watch them and they were never like this" Patricia said clearly less than chuffed with my attitude to Darlene. But Darlene was my sister and she needed telling she wouldn't understand if I didn't shout at her, it's the only way to get anything through to her, you need to shout so that she can hear you above the voices in her head that are telling her she is a princess and everything she does is okay.

"Aye Danny stop shouting at me" Darlene said as she looked at Patricia, not clear whether Patricia was slagging her or supporting her by saying she couldn't cope.

As she had stopped shouting so did I "Where is John" I asked, not shouting but still smouldering.

"The wean?" Darlene asked looking puzzled.

"No, not the wean you half-wit, your useless excuse for a man" I shouted.

"So much for you not shouting" Darlene said "He's pissed off with some tart" she added.

Patricia gasped and said "When? Do you know her?"

I answered for Darlene "There isn't a when, he has been doing it since before they were married and ever since and she knows some of them, her pals her neighbours and once even her cousin. Everybody knows about it but nobody is supposed to mention in because her ladyship here denies it and goes in a huff with everybody and threatens never to speak to them again if they say anything to him," I looked straight into Darlene's eyes daring her to call me a liar, she dropped her head.

"Why do you put up with this shit, let me break his legs or let Charlie stab him or something you know he wants to and get him to fuck out of your life" I said earnestly and without anger.

128

"You'se canny do that, you'se will go to jail" Patricia said with sweet naivety.

"It's only people stupid enough to get caught that go to jail" I said looking at Darlene for approval.

"He still loves me" she said "He just needs a lot of sex, that's all that's wrong with him, they other lassies are just for sex, it's me he loves, did you notice if there was any vodka left in that bottle in the bedroom or did I leave it in here?" I struggled to control my tongue, she was hurt enough without me making it worse by shouting at her, I lost the struggle.

"What are you a complete moron, he is a user and a womaniser, I can solve his problem with needing lots of sex I can cut off his dick and stuff it up his arse" I screamed at her "This time you aren't talking me out of it" I stood to go, I was already planning how to tell Charlie we needed somewhere to bury a six foot two inch body.

"Danny sit down and control yourself, you screaming at her really isnae helping anybody" Patricia said and she was absolutely right it wasn't, so I did the most sensible thing, I screamed at her as well.

"Don't sit and listen to her shite, this bastard has had it coming for years and his time is up. You are just as stupid as her if you give in to her" I said and instantly regretted my stupid mouth. Patricia looked as if I had slapped her, it wasn't the first time I had shouted at her but it was probably the first time with venom and it showed. Not that it mattered to me because I was angry, really angry. I cleared the cups and ashtrays that were on the kitchen table with a single sweep of my arm, they all crashed into the wall and fell to the floor in pieces. I had a flashback to my Da throwing his plate of stew and potato's at my Ma and it crashing into the wall above her head and the stew running down the wall behind her. I stood watching tea run down Darlene's wall and shivered slightly.

"Right, okay, okay" I said to Patricia. I could see I had scared her. I took a couple of minutes to calm down as Patricia leaned down to pick up the pieces of broken crockery.

"Just leave them hen, it hardly makes a difference in here does it?" Darlene said as she spread her arms indicating the rest of the kitchen with dirty dishes and takeaway cartons strewn on every surface.

"Darlene you need to pack up your stuff and go to my Ma's with the weans. Look at the state of this place, there isnae even any electric, the place hasn't seen a mop or a brush for a month if ever, it looks like. Get back to bed and I will bring the weans up in the morning and we can take a walk down to my Ma's." I said now calmed and reasonable.

Darlene laughed "I don't walk, I take taxi's and anyway I'm not running back to my Ma she hates John and will just be all 'I told you' at me, and Dorothy will be the same, she was screaming at me after your wedding to jail him, leave him or stab him, or all three but just to do something with him. No, I'm not going to my Ma's. He will be home tomorrow and I will tell him that this is his last chance and one more woman or one more slap and he is history, I don't need him and I will tell him that" she said with her usual brand of defiance.

"You're a complete idiot Darlene and you probably deserve everything you get. If you thinks this is the kind of life you want then just keep it, but is this really all you are worth? Nobody can help you if you won't help yourself. Come on Patricia, I'm tired and this is a waste of time. I will bring the weans up tomorrow, I should just keep them or hand them in to the social, but I will bring them back tomorrow and you can torture them a bit more." I said rising to go.

"Don't let the door hit your arse on the way out" Darlene said looking around the kitchen, presumably for her lost dregs of vodka.

We took the kids back at lunchtime the next day, and to our complete surprise Darlene was up and dressed. Made up to the nines as if she was going to the disco.

"We're moving" she said as she continued to stuff dirty clothes into a battered suitcase.

"Moving where" I asked picking wee Charlene up and cuddling her.

"Coventry" Darlene said.

"Ventry" Charlene said.

I smiled at Charlene and kissed her cheek and asked Darlene "What's in Coventry and I presume you are taking the weans"

"John has got family in Coventry, they can get us a house down there and John has got a job lined up and I can get a job as well if I want" she said hurriedly.

"See this house in Coventry" I asked "Is it a wee white cottage with a white fence round the garden and rose bushes at either side of the door?" I looked at her waiting for a response.

"You're really funny Danny, well done, ha ha, there you go, are you satisfied I laughed at your joke? Is that what you want? We are starting again okay, he has got family down there, and it worked for Dot. Look how she's getting on in Redcar. She's got her own house now with a garden and all that, why shouldn't I get the same, do I not deserve it or something?" She started to cry, Patricia threw me a look clearly blaming me for everything that was wrong with Darlene, and by the look of it Maggie thatcher was maybe my fault as well.

I shrugged my shoulders and said to wee John and Charlene come on we will go to the shops and get some sweeties you'se are going in the car with daddy for a wee holiday.

"Gonny put a nappy on Charlene first Danny, she's only got a wee pair of pants on." Patricia said.

"There isn't any clean nappies" Darlene said going into her purse and handing me a fiver, "I was gonny get a pack of them disposable ones until I get settled in with a washing machine and that"

I grabbed the money from her and took wee john to the shops with me and left Charlene with Patricia and Darlene. I took my time because I was still angry and didn't really want to argue with Darlene again, it was getting neither of us anywhere. When I got back Darlene with Patricia's help had finished her packing she had two battered suitcases and four black bin bags lined up in the hall ready to go.

"So where is he then?" I asked Darlene "The man of the moment big John Lawson"

"Don't start Danny" Patricia said.

Darlene added "Aye don't start on him Danny, if you fight him he would give you a doing, he's much bigger than you and he can fight you canny" She had a point, I was a better talker than a fighter but my bad temper usually got me over the line. Although to be honest John Lawson wasn't really that great a fighter and I would have been happy to take him on as long as I had a hammer tucked into my waistband or Charlie at my back. But with his two kids and Darlene being there it wasn't the time or the place.

"I'm not going to start anything" I said "I'm heading down to the bookies to see if I can get a shift, when he disnae even bother turning up to get you Darlene, come and get me and I will give you a walk down to my Ma's if I'm not working" I left Patricia with her.

I couldn't get a shift but stayed in the bookies all afternoon anyway, it was better than sitting in Patricia's Ma's and doing nothing even if the one pound forty I had in my pocket was gone after two races. I regularly popped my head out of the door to see if I could spot Lawson turning up. I obviously missed him because about two hours later Patricia came to fetch me. He had indeed turned up in a fancy car, bundled Darlene, the weans and their meagre possessions into it and driven off. I was relieved in a way to have missed his departure.

"So what happened then, are they going to Coventry?" I asked Patricia who was still annoyed at me, I could tell the way she slapped my arm when I cuddled her and grabbed her bum.

"Aye they have" she said pushing me away "And Darlene said we could take anything we wanted out of her house, because it is a lot of tat and if we want it we can have it"

"Aye that's what we need a load of broken stuff hoaching with fleas" I said dismissing the idea.

"Actually Danny for somebody that thinks their smart you aren't really. Right now we have nothing to sit on, nothing to sleep on, nothing to cook on, nothing to walk on, and nothing to wash our clothes with. So is it better to have nothing or better to go and see what Darlene had and if any of it is worth keeping" Patricia said arms folded in her habitual don't mess with me stance.

"That's what I meant, that maybe whatever she is leaving would be better than nothing, even if it's hoaching with fleas, what did you think I meant" I asked smiling as I walked past her and slapped her bum and said "Come on, we might as well have a look" She just shook her head but at least she added a smile.

We spent the rest of that day salvaging whatever we could from Darlene's house, we took the cooker, even though we couldn't check whether it was working or not because there was no electricity. When we got it into our kitchen we found out that two of the four rings were working as well as the eye level grill and the oven, so that was a good result. Patricia reckoned it would be a full time job to get it clean but so be it.
We took her couch even though the middle seat had broken below the cushion and if you sat on it you fell through to the floor, but it looked reasonably okay, if maybe a bit dirty, so I went out into the back court and found a bit of plywood which I cut and placed under the middle cushion, so if you were careful it was okay to sit on, although you did sink into it slightly. We took all of her curtains and netting and curtain wires. My Ma let us wash all the curtains and netting in her washing machine and hang them in the back court at Cessnock to dry, but it was October so they didn't dry very well. We took them back up to McCulloch Street in an old pram, my Ma used to use for taking her washing to the laundrette before we had a washing machine.

It was a hard slog pushing a pram up Shields Road full of soaking wet curtains, and it didn't really help matters when it started pouring with rain, but we treated it as a laugh and an adventure which it clearly was. When we had taken everything that was possible to take from Darlene's house and added it to the other stuff that people had gave us we ended up with a house that had most things it needed to live in, although we had neither a television or a washing machine.

On the nights Patricia wasn't working we would go visiting anybody and everybody. One night it would be her ma the next night it would be mine. Then some other night we would walk to Pollok from Pollokshields a good ten mile return trip and visit Donnie, Annie and all the weans. Annie now had five and they were all blue eyed blonde beauties and they could all giggle for Scotland. We even occasionally visited Dunky in his flat in Govan, usually to find him with a different woman in tow each time we arrived. We also visited Patricia's sister a couple of times a week.

The visiting had more than one purpose, of course I was missing everybody, and it was a big change for me, moving out of the hustle and bustle of my Ma's house and into a room and kitchen with only Patricia and me in it. But just as important when we were visiting our families it meant we weren't burning electricity or using up our meagre supplies of tea bags and sugar. It wasn't deliberate but it did help because I was still refusing to sign on and most of Patricia's wages went on rent.

Charlie eventually forced me to sign on and to use the system to whatever advantage I could. He went with me and told me how to apply for a grant for furniture and bedding as well as just about everything else you needed to start a new house. He helped me move all of the stuff I did own into a neighbour's house when the social came to inspect my house and what I had to see if I qualified for a hardship grant or not. They ended up giving me over six hundred pounds, an unbelievable amount of money just in time for Christmas. Charlie knew their system better than they did, he would come with me whenever I applied for anything and tell whoever was interviewing me what page of their guidelines I was claiming under and would list all the reasons why they had to grant my application.

So we got a telly, albeit a coin operated one from Radio Rentals, we didn't want to waste our money buying one but at least we could afford the six pound deposit to rent one. We also got a second hand twin tub from a shop in Albert drive, it had seen better days and leaked a bit when it was spinning but we just put some towels down on the linoleum and it was fine. We also put linoleum all through the house, we couldn't afford carpet so linoleum was better than floorboards. We decorated both rooms and the bathroom with wallpaper. Which I hung by myself, I had helped my da a few times so was reasonably sure I could handle it.

Patricia helped me wallpaper the living room but refused to help me with any more rooms because when doing the living room I had come to a particularly difficult corner, where I had to stand on a ladder and cut the paper diagonally to make it fit, And I had to do this with a full length strip of paper with paste on it. The first time I tried it the paper split across the middle and fell to the floor in two halves. The second time I tried it I fell off the ladder and wrapped the pasted paper around me. When my reaction to that was to tear the paper to shreds throw my paste brush at the wall, kick the stepladder to the floor and scream obscenities at the wallpaper, Patricia said she wasn't helping me anymore I was a lunatic and too scary, personally I couldn't see her problem. But probably shouldn't have told her to fuck off back to her Ma's then.

I eventually finished the wallpapering and painting a week before Christmas, we still had most of the furniture from Darlene's but we had a telly a new picture above the fireplace and a new coffee table, we also had a Christmas tree and some baubles to hang on it. The only thing we agreed we would have liked but couldn't afford was a carpet for the living room or at least a big rug, because it would have made it much cosier.

So I was delighted a couple of nights later when I spotted Patricia's Granda, Jock the Plum, coming along my street pushing an old fruit barrow with a rolled up carpet on it. Jock was an old retired docker but nowadays he spent his time mooching about the Barra's and the Briggait, two old fashioned street markets where you could buy or sell practically anything. He had told Patricia and me the week before when we had been visiting him that he would keep an eye out for a carpet for us. Obviously he had found something.

I went into the street to meet him.

"Here you go Donnie, I found this wee carpet for you" he said trying to get his shoulder under the middle of it and lift it all by himself.

"It's Danny, Jock and let me help you with that" I said going to one end and getting it on to my shoulder.

"Aye okay Donnie" he says and gets the other end onto his shoulder, it was heavy so must be a good size I thought, it also had plenty of brown tape round it holding it in place. As I carried it in I must have stood on

135

some dogshit and had to try and scrape it off my feet before I got into the house. So I swerved slightly towards some grass by the side of our close, I think I managed to scrape it off, it was dark but I could smell it.

Jock helped me into the hallway and we put the carpet down and asked if I wanted help moving the furniture about so I could roll the carpet out. I declined because it was after nine o'clock and I had to go and meet Patricia when she finished in the bingo at ten. Since Patricia worked in the bingo at the end of the street Jock lived in, it made sense to walk him home. So I grabbed my jacket and offered to walk Jock down the road. I kept stopping all the way down the road to try and scrape the dogshit from my shoe because I could still smell it.

Jock took the opportunity to tell me a story that he would later tell me more than one hundred times over the twenty odd years I knew him.

"Did I tell you Donnie about the time I was on manoeuvres in a big cemetery up at Dundee before the war" He asked casually with a grin on his face as we walked briskly in an effort to keep out the cold, I had offered to push the handcart but he was happy to do so.

"No Jock, you didnae tell me about it and by the way my name's still danny, Donnie is my big brother the one that's married to Annie, your daughter Betty's best pal" I said in an effort to get him to stop calling me Donnie, it made me feel older and shorter.

"What wee Annie with the red hair and the huge bazoomba's?" he asked leaving the hand cart go to use his hands to illustrate what he meant by bazoomba's.
"Aye Jock, my sister in law with the big bazoomba's that's right, Donnie's married to her. I'm married to your granddaughter Patricia, also with the big..." I thought better of finishing that sentence.

"Eh?" he asked.

"Nothing Jock, tell me about when you were on manoeuvres at that big cemetery in Dundee before the war" I said trying to cover up my faux pas of telling him about the size of his granddaughter's bazoomba's.

"How do you know about that?" he asked suspiciously "Did somebody tell you about it"

I looked closely at him to see if he was taking the pish, he didn't appear to be. "You told me about it Jock a couple of minutes ago" I said slowly and clearly, since I had now decided he was off his head.

"Aye, that was a right funny tale wasn't it" he said and started laughing so much he had to stop pushing the cart and bend over, "Aye that was the funniest thing ever wasn't it?" he asked with tears of laughter still on his cheek.

"You never told me about it Jock" I said.

"You just said I did son, are you taking the pish. I can still give you the old one two son, don't worry about that" he said letting go of the handcart and taking up a boxers stance and demonstrating not only his one two but his right cross left cross and uppercut as well. Each swing of his hands getting closer and closer to my face.

"Whoa, wait a minute Jock, you never told me the full story, you told me you were gonnae tell me the story and you haven't yet" I said dodging his wild blows. He might be near seventy but he was as strong as a horse and just as big.

"What story?" he said

And when I said "Oh for fucks sake" he laughed like a loony and said "I got you there wee man didn't I" I had to laugh along with him he had indeed got me there.

"Right, wee man, there we are me and Tommy Gilgannon blacked up and in full nigh time combat gear. We have to make our way across this huge big cemetery just outside Dundee without being spotted. So we have to crawl between headstones and under bushes and all sorts. We are about half way across when Tommy digs his rifle into my ribs and uses it to point at something. I give him a hard stare, getting the butt of a rifle in the ribs is bloody sore. But I have a look at what he is pointing at and all I can see is somebody lying on a bench beside a path between the gravestones. So tommy motions to me to follow him and keep quiet. The bench is only

137

about fifty yards away from us but it's quite out in the open so we have to circle around him until we are behind two headstones, which are only a few feet behind the bench."

I looked at him as he pushed the handcart and told his story and could see the merriment in his eyes and realised that he wasn't with me. He was back there in that cemetery as if it had been yesterday.

"So I look at tommy and gestures to him with a what now gesture and Tommy goes 'whoooooo' like a ghost but quite quietly. I look at him as if he is an eejit and he does it again. And then I saw the guy on the bench sit up as if somebody stuck something up his arse. 'Who's that' he shouts out and starts swivelling round to see what he can see. And it turns out it's just an old tramp, half drunk and half sleeping, and he keeps looking in every direction at once trying to see what made the noise.

Well he canny see us, a German with a snipers scope wouldn't have been able to see us. So he lies down again and then I go, 'Whooooooo, there's nobody here but me and you' then he sits up again, terrified he was. He starts fumbling about under the bench and there are loads of sheets of newspaper flying everywhere, he must have been using them as his blanket. He's still fumbling about for something down at his feet so I do it again 'Whoooooo, there's nobody here but me and you' and he shouts out 'if you give me a fucking minute to find my boots there'll be nobody here but you yourself' and then he picks up his boots one in each hand and runs like a wee fat bastard all the way down the hill and climbs over the fence. He must have fell three times on the way down that hill and he had to run across a gravel path to get to the fence and we could hear him going ooh aah all the way across it, the funniest sight I ever seen in my life" he said and went off into more howls of laughter, I joined in not just because it was funny but also because of his sheer joy in the telling of the story.

During the hundred or so times he told me that story he laughed just as hard every single time, as did I. We parted ways at the paisley road toll, he had to go over towards the Barra's to return the handcart he shook my hand and wished me 'all the best Donnie'.

I was still smiling when I met Patricia outside her work at half past ten, despite finishing at ten she always manages to be last out of the building, I accused her having reflection constipation once and then I explained that it meant unable to pass a mirror.

I told her about her Granda dropping off a carpet for us and that she could help me move the living room furniture when we got home and we would lay it out. She looked dubiously at me as if I was joking and eventually she believed me that I was serious. She also asked me if I had stepped in dogshit, I stopped at a wee wall outside Jim Baxter's pub at the toll, and took my shoes off, there was nothing on the bottom of them at all.

We almost ran up the road we were both keen to see if the carpet was any good, it was the one thing we thought we needed for the living room. We opened the front door to an awful smell.

"Oh for god's sake Danny, did you drag in whatever it was you stood on and just wipe it on the floor in here" Patricia said boaking and running out of the house.

"No I didnae" I said vehemently. I could have I suppose but I wasn't going to admit it.

"Then it must be that minging carpet, did my Granda say where he got it?" she asked eying me with suspicion as if it was me that had done something wrong.

"No he didnae say anything, just that he had picked up a nice bit of carpet because you had asked him to" I said defensively.

"I never asked him anything, you must have" she said "Anyway it disnae matter just get it out of my house" she said "Right now" she added with meaning.

It was a heavy bit of carpet and it took me a wee while to drag it out of the house, and since I couldn't open it in the close I dragged it out to the street and opened it there, after going in and getting a Stanley knife. The house didn't smell any better with the carpet out than it had with it in. Despite the fact it was almost midnight our comings and goings had attracted an audience of five or six of our neighbours, which was always the way in McCulloch Street, it could be four in the morning in a snowstorm and there would still be somebody at their window looking out to see if anything was happening.

After I had cut all the straps of brown tape holding the carpet in a roll, I mimicked a drum roll as I kicked the carpet to make it roll out flat, it stuck somewhere near the middle so I gave it another kick to complete the job. Our suspicions were proved right, there was a fair amount of dogshit right in the middle of the carpet, but I am pretty sure that what was actually causing the god awful smell was the dead dog that was there as well.

Patricia ran across the road away from it dry boaking as she went, the two other women went with her and me and the four guys went a bit closer to see what kind of dog it was. I wished my wee brother Paul was with me, he would have loved this, since he was a grotty wee shit at the best of times. It looked just like a wee mongrel, it was a shame. Two of the guys watching helped me roll the carpet up and dump it over the fence into the primary school playground which was opposite my house. I know we shouldn't have but the jannie would take care of it in the morning before any weans got near it. Probably.

Patricia came back across the road and said "It's still minging over here, what's it going to be like inside the house"

"No worse than when you fart, I would imagine" I said, the two guys standing beside me found that funnier than Patricia did.

"What did the dog die with" she asked me.

"I'm not sure, I never did an autopsy but probably because it had stopped breathing and its heart had stopped beating, that's what usually kills things" I said sarcastically.

"Just like you in about twenty minutes you mean, or as soon as you fall asleep you sarcastic bastard. Come on get in the house before anybody else sees what you did with that carpet." She said grabbing my arm and pulling me. "You are still absolutely stinking" she added "Has some of that got on your jacket?"

"I don't think so" I said feeling both of my shoulders as we went in the front door. Then I remembered I didn't have my Jacket on when I helped

140

jock the Plum carry the carpet in, I took my jacket off and felt the shoulder of my pullover, and it was very wet. And then Patricia who was standing behind me screamed. The back of my nice white Christmas jumper was soaked in blood. Cheers jock merry Christmas to you as well.

## Chapter twenty four;   Daddy Danny the scaffolder.

"What is it?" I asked pushing the covers back slightly so I could see what time it was, it was half past one in the morning, on the second of January 1981. I was still recovering from the first of January and had only been in bed less than an hour. "Who is it?" I shouted somebody was banging on the window beside my bed. I looked round it was my wee brother Paul, what the hell did he want at this time in the morning?

I opened the window letting in a blast of icy air and causing a blast of icy language from Patricia. But I told her it was easier to open the window and drag Paul in rather than walk to the front door some fifteen feet away, she disagreed. Strongly.

"What's the matter, do you know what time it is, this better be good, I'm telling you" I said.

"Charlie has been on the phone to my Ma's house, he is fighting with some of his neighbours he wants you to go up and bring some pals" Paul said breathlessly, he had run up all the way from Cessnock.

"Pals, what pals, I don't have pals I have brothers" I shouted at Paul needlessly. What had Charlie got himself into now? I ran all the way back down to Cessnock with Paul and roused searcher and big Bobby out of their beds which they weren't chuffed with but accepted as part of the price you paid to know Charlie. I couldn't imagine that we would need any more than us four so I persuaded searcher to pay for the taxi out to Castlemilk where Charlie had got his first house. Paul desperately tried to get into the taxi with us and I had to actually slap him to stop him from coming. I had no idea what we were getting into and he was only thirteen or something, I couldn't imagine what my Ma would do to me if he got hurt because of my stupidity. He even ran after the taxi for a few hundred yards, searcher tried to persuade the taxi driver to slow down and see how far we could get him to follow us. I told the driver to put the boot down and warned Searcher not to take the piss.

We got to Charlie's house at almost half past three and there was a crowd of about ten guys hanging about in his garden and at his front gate. I had underestimated the problem apparently but then again maybe not. Charlie had seen us arriving, he was standing at an upstairs window. I didn't see him but I saw the curtains twitch and ten seconds later he was out of his front door a butcher's knife in one hand and a length of wood in the other and he started swinging wildly at the ten guys in his garden. A few seconds later we were all out of the taxi and into the fray.

At least half of them ran at the first onslaught and the ones that remained were soon begging for it to be over. I had to pull Charlie away from the final two, he was determined to stab at least one of them, despite the fact that they were both cowering under the hedge at the foot of his garden with what looked like quite serious cuts on their faces.

"Where are Iris and wee Charlie?" I asked, after telling Searcher to get the two guys out from under the hedge and away from here as I couldn't hold on to Charlie much longer.

Before I could answer Iris appeared at the front door with the wean in one arm and two kit bags full of clothes and possessions in the other. I turned round and amazingly enough the taxi was still there. Not really that surprising I suppose, we hadn't paid him yet. The taxi driver chuckled most of the way to the Gorbals, where we were going to drop Iris and the wean at her Ma's. He said that at least two of the guys who had bolted the moment Charlie came out of his house tooled up could represent Scotland at the Olympics they were that fast. Although he wasn't sure if it was Charlie with a sword or the sight of the gorilla getting out of the taxi that made them bolt in the first place. "No offence big man" he said to big Bobby.

We dropped Iris and continued on to Cessnock the plan now was to borrow my Da's van without him knowing, even though none of us had a licence both Searcher and Charlie were good drivers and had been driving since they were fourteen. And then go back to Castlemilk and get all of Charlie's furniture and stuff. The taxi driver wanted fifteen quid for the journey, probably because that's what it said on the meter, I suppose. Searcher argued with him that he shouldn't have charged waiting time while the fight was going on, because in fact we had entertained him more than going to the pictures would have.

The driver told him that he would get out of his cab and take all four of us on if we didn't cough up. \he was probably about sixty or something but I believed him. Charlie told searcher to give the guy twenty quid for his troubles and that he would square Searcher up when we got all of his belongings including his wallet back when we got to Castlemilk. Searcher quite rightly observed that he had a better chance of seeing the Loch Ness monster than of ever seeing that twenty quid again. I didn't mention that I had seen iris hand Charlie his wallet when we got into the taxi, it was none of my business.

We did borrow my Da's van and this time we allowed Paul to come with us, mostly because he had crawled quietly into my Da's room and nicked the keys for us. But we never got any of Charlie's stuff anyway, when we got to Castlemilk there were now about twenty guys in the garden and a load of women and kids in the house carrying everything of any value out and smashing all of the windows as they went along.

It was like watching locusts stripping a field of corn. As Charlie drove the van past them, Paul wound the window down and told them they were a bunch of thieving pricks and that we would be back with the Govan team. Searcher slapped him across the back of the head shouting at him, "This heap of shit van only does about ten miles an hour they could probably run after us and catch us if they wanted, you half-wit" Ordinarily I wouldn't allow anybody to call my wee brother a half-wit but since he was, I let it go. Charlie never got any of his stuff back, of course, and despite Paul's warning we never went back with the Govan team. Mainly because none of were in the Govan team and in fact had spent at least the previous three or four years fighting with some of the Govan team, big Bobby had a huge scar on his back to prove it, which was Searcher's fault but that's a different story.

When I eventually got home Patricia was livid with me. "You canny keep getting out of bed in the middle of the night and disappearing to god knows where and leaving me sitting up all night worrying" she said with righteous anger.

"How no?" I answered with a grin.

"Because it's no fair, you could be dead or anything, for all I know" she said seemingly genuinely worried.

I gave her a wee cuddle and gave her bum a wee squeeze "Okay" I said "In future I will take somebody with me and send them back to tell you what's happening, or when we are rich we can get a phone put in, Did you really stay up all night worrying about me baby" I asked grabbing another squeeze at her bum and trying to put my hand up her jumper.

"No" she said pushing me away "but I could have for all you cared"

The following week brought good news and some other news that we would need to wait and see if it was good or bad. The good news was that my Da had got me a job beside him as a scaffolder, I had to turn up and look like a scaffolder and pretend to be a scaffolder if anybody asked me, I could do that. The job was in Edinburgh, they were building a shopping centre at Cameron toll, it was a big job and my Da was in charge of all the scaffolder's which was about forty men fifteen of us were to go over from Glasgow every day in a minibus and the rest were local guys. The deal was that I had to catch the first subway every morning from Shields road to Cowcaddens and the minibus would be waiting for me.

The news that we would have to get used to before we decided whether it was good or bad was that Charlie was moving in next door to us. He had been visiting me the week before and noticed that the flat next door to me was empty. The flat I lived in was half of a house really, our room and kitchen faced the street and the other half of the house which was also a room and kitchen faced the back court. Both flats shared a front door called a storm door in the close, once inside that front door both flats then had their own front door. When he had noticed the flat was empty he went straight to the West of Scotland housing association and asked for it on the basis that iris and he were homeless and were in fact sleeping on my living room floor. Which they weren't but when had the truth ever got a chance to spoil a Charlie tale.

Patricia and Iris got along okay, but they were never going to be best friends. I suppose the problem being that every time I was in any bother Patricia blamed Charlie and if Charlie was in any bother I seemed to be near at hand so Iris maybe blamed me. But then again Patricia got on great with Charlie and Iris got on great with me, it was just each other they rubbed up the wrong way.

But that could sort itself out the main thing was that I had a full time job with great wages, and a chance to make Patricia happy, within half an hour of my Da telling me about the job, Patricia had picked out the carpets and curtains she wanted for our living room.

The first three days at my new job went great, I caught the first subway got off at Cowcaddens and hopped on the minibus. At the job site all the Glasgow guys knew the score, they had to make out I was a scaffolder the same as them because I was on the same money as them, but if any of the local guys found out that I wasn't really a scaffolder they could kick up a stink. On the very first day the local guys sussed it out in fact they sussed it after about half an hour when I didn't know what a 'Paddy' was, it turns out it was a twenty foot scaffolding tube. A paddy McGinty being rhyming slang for twenty.
It never bothered anybody, scaffolders were a protective breed, to their own and they accepted me as one of their own, made easier by my old man being the gaffer I dare say. They were also predominantly mad, they considered themselves the bravest men on any site, even braver than the steel erectors and superior to all other tradesmen, their favourite saying was that god invented scaffolders so that brickies had someone to idolise.

On the third day we stopped at a pub after we got off the minibus at Cowcaddens and Dunky slipped me a tenner to stand my corner which I never got to spend because all of the older guys wanted to buy me my first pint as a scaffolder. I got drunk, very drunk. Which was the prime reason I woke up in a panic at six o'clock in the morning. I had four minutes to get to the subway station if I was to catch the first train. I made a great effort, running down the stairs onto the platform just as the arse end of the train was leaving the station. The next train was seven minutes later, surely my Da would hold the mini bus back for seven minutes, the answer to that is no he wouldn't. When I got to Cowcaddens and the minibus was gone I got into a mini panic, my Da would be raging, he expected Donnie Dunky and me to be absolutely perfect and the best at anything we had to do at work, he drove us harder than anybody else and always gave us the hardest jobs to do, we were McCallister's and had to be better than anybody else.

145

One thing I was good at was thinking on my feet, I sprinted back into the subway and went to Queen Street railway station and caught a train to Edinburgh Waverley, the train was due into Waverley Station at seven forty, so if I could get a taxi from there to Cameron toll there was a slight chance I would be on site before my Da, how funny would that be? And the train and taxi gods smiled on me, I got to the site a good ten minutes before the minibus was due. I decided to get the portacabin opened up the gas heater and the tea urn fired up and be sitting with my feet up and a cup of tea in my hand before my Da arrived.

All of which I managed but by ten past eight the minibus still hadn't arrived, by half past eight I was getting a bit worried and strolled down to the entrance gate and into the security hut. The security man who I knew by name because he was an ex scaffolder and usually came to our portacabin for a cup of tea in the morning before we started, really just to swap old war stories with my Da I think, was surprised to see me.

"What are you doing here son, you're big Davie's boy eh?" He said looking up from his newspaper.

That was a bit of a strange question, I was here to work, to build scaffolding why else would I be there.

"I'm waiting for my Da and the rest of the squad" I said looking out of his hut window down the main road.

"Are you?" he asked again with surprise on his face "When did they start working Saturdays on this job then?"

My heart sank, it was Saturday, no wonder there was nobody at Cowcaddens we didn't work Saturdays. I wished a hole would open up and swallow me, this old bastard was already laughing. I bet he couldn't wait until Monday to tell everybody how I turned up in a taxi sweating like a thief in a police station. I don't think he believed me when I said my Da wanted me in to tidy up all the tools and the cabin and that I had just thought the rest of them were getting overtime as well, even though I spent a couple of hours doing just that before tapping him for a fiver to get home. By Monday when everybody was taking the piss out of me I knew he hadn't believed me.

Charlie and Iris moved in next door and by and large it was fine. We baby sat for them a few times and wee Charlie was brilliant, although we only watched him overnight a few times and at first I sat up beside his cot for the whole night and nudged him every time I thought he wasn't breathing loud enough. I loved watching the wee man and so did Patricia, but only during the day, she wasn't a 'during the night' type of person, during the night had only one purpose in her life, and that was sleeping. And during the night for her was from two am until eleven am, she had no problem staying up until two in the morning but eleven o'clock in the morning was her preferred 'waking up' time. So whenever we did mind wee Charlie I got the pleasure of any night time feeds, but I didn't care, there is nothing as good as watching a wean taking a four o'clock bottle of warm milk and going from screaming banshee to contented burping. Although the shitty nappies wee Charlie produced were not so sweet.

Everything settled down nicely for the next couple of months, I was earning good money, Patricia still had her bingo money. I started playing for a pub darts team in the Quaich bar on Paisley road along with Donnie, Dunky and Charlie as usual with us it was very competitive, and as usual I was probably the worst of the four of us. I hadn't yet been able to find anything that I was the best at.
We were ultra-competitive at everything and I mean everything.

Back when Charlie and I had been about thirteen and fifteen we had seen some table tennis on The world of Sport one Saturday afternoon and decided we wanted a go at that it looked good. So we bought a packet of ping pong balls from The Sports Emporium which was straight across the road from us on the corner of Percy Street. We got the fold down leaf table out of the living room and put it in the hall, we the used six or seven hardback books opened slightly so that they would stand up all across the table to act as the net. Since we didn't have bats we cut bat shapes from the hard covers of other books at first but eventually cut square bats from a sheet of plywood that as in the coal bunker doing nothing. Charlie even glued some felt cloth he nicked from school to the bats, which we convinced ourselves made them look professional and helped us to spin the ball, the way the Chinese guys did on the telly.

From then on Saturday afternoons in my Ma's consisted of a table tennis tournament. Even Donnie and Dunky would delay going to the pub on a Saturday afternoon to make sure they could play in the tournament.

Occasionally some of our friends would join us but inevitably it came down to any two of the McCallister brothers in the final and this was contested as if it was the world cup final or the punishment for losing was death. More often than not a fistfight would erupt either during or after the game and even on the odd occasion before the game had even started, usually over the result of the previous week's game.

Charlie and I played incessantly during the week which allowed us to become better than both Dunky and Donnie, so most of the finals were eventually between us. That table tennis table came out almost every day for over a year. For Christmas that year wee Paul got a table tennis set of bats and a net, which renewed everybody's enthusiasm for the game, eventually we all purchased our own high quality thick bats and wrote our names on the handles convinced that we were better with our own bat and blaming any bad shots or games we had on not having our own bat.

The table tennis frenzy only really stopped when Charlie and I had moved out and my Da decided to build a pool table in the big bedroom that had formerly held four beds. This idea came about when he found a couple of large squares of slate on a site he was working on. He decided that he could build a pool table around them and he did. He cut two one inch thick sheets of plywood, again 'found' on a building site and sandwiched the slate between them, he made legs from some lengths of four by two. He used the same lengths of four by two to form the 'cushion' part of the table. He bought some rubber trim to act as the actual 'cushion' which annoyed him because it was the first thing he had had to buy, he had been hoping to be able to boast about building it for nothing. But he also had to buy the roll of felt cloth so now he boasted that he had built the table for four pounds forty eight pence exactly. And the strangest thing was that it sort of worked, it wasn't as good as a pub table and the balls sometimes bounced off at odd angles, and maybe it wasn't great getting the balls out of the football socks he had used to provide 'pockets' but so what. We must have been one of the first families in Govan to have our own pool table. So pool took over as the game of choice and the table tennis tournaments were consigned to history. Which wasn't great for me, everybody was better at pool than me.

That's not to say I wasn't any good, just that the rest of them were very good even Paul and wee David got better than me quite quickly. In fact there was an occasion when my Da, with drunken bravado challenged the top team at a local snooker hall to a challenge match for a stake of a hundred pounds, we beat them seven matches to one, with me being the only one to lose.

So from being a regular finalist in the table tennis tournament, I became almost a spectator at the Saturday pool tournaments. But the upside was that the post final fights were now usually between Donnie and Charlie, which were mostly arguments rather than full blown fights, Dunky and I could usually intervene before the blows started flying. All McCallister's are competitive and love to win but Donnie and Charlie took being a bad loser to new heights. They were never gracious in defeat, never ever, if they lost it was always somebody else's fault.

Either they had been cheated or they had been unlucky or they had faulty equipment be it blunt darts or a bent pool queue but almost always it wasn't that their opponent had been better, it was that they had been hard done to. This came to a ridiculous point one day years later when I was playing Donnie at scrabble and he accused me of learning to read braille so that when my hand was in the bag choosing Scrabble tiles I could feel what they were and that was the reason I kept beating him with seven letter words.

The pool table was not the only thing that came from building sites to my Ma's house. My Da came home once with a huge roll of lovely red carpet, very thick and luxurious red carpet which had a monogrammed capital M across it in rows every yard or so. The M was for McCallister he told my Ma until she seen the same carpet in Woolworths in the city centre and realised that the M was actually an upside down W. It was still the highest quality carpet we had ever had, and was down in the hall until my Ma and Da left the house a few years later.

My Da explained to me while we worked on the site at The Cameron Toll shopping centre together that everybody nicked things from the site, it was a perk of the job. He introduced me to a guy called Ramsay Thompson, who took this to extremes. Ramsay was a very interesting man, he told magnificent stories. He was in his mid to late fifties a couple of years older than my Da and he told me one day that he had lost the use of his legs for eight years when he was about twenty one, he had woken up one morning unable to walk and the doctors and hospitals couldn't explain why and then one day eight years later he woke up able to walk again. Naturally I accused him of talking crap and making it up, he eventually convinced me it was true, I was always waiting for a punch-line but it never came.

Ramsay built a four bedroom two bathroomed bungalow on the outskirts of Stirling entirely with material nicked from the Cameron Toll shopping centre. This wasn't a story he made up. This was fact and I know it was fact because not only did I help him finish off his lawn at the back of the house, I spoke to the brickies, plumbers, joiners, glaziers, roofers and electricians who provided the materials and did the work building it. He paid them all double time as long as they brought the materials he needed with them free of charge, so brickies would turn up with a couple of pallets of bricks and work a full weekend overtime for cash in hand. He told me to keep quiet about it but he reckoned he had built that four bedroomed bungalow in more than an acre of grounds for less than three thousand pounds, excluding the cost of the land which was another two thousand. I was at the house warming party with about sixty other guys who all had a hand in building Ramsay Thompson's stunningly beautiful house. I only worked with Ramsay for about six months but I don't think I ever met anyone more interesting in my life.

The first eight months in our new house flew in, but Patricia and me really only seen each other at the weekends. From April onwards we worked late most nights at the building site and Patricia was still working until after ten at the bingo, so by the time she came in from work I was ready for bed. I still walked down to the bingo most nights to meet her and we would walk up to McCulloch Street, except for Tuesday nights. I played darts on a Tuesday night so that night Patricia would walk from the bingo to the Quaich bar and meet me and then we would walk home. On one particular Tuesday she did just that, but we didn't go straight home, her Ma had been at the bingo with her granny that night and asked Patricia to go up to her house on the way home and take the dog out for a walk.

Describing Shep as a dog is a bit on the generous side it was more like a wire toilet brush with teeth and a tail. I have no idea what type of dog it was supposed to be. I do know that I didn't like it and it didn't particularly like me. The main reason I didn't like it was because it never felt like a dog, you should be able to pet a dog and rub its coat and get some satisfaction from that. When rubbing Shep you were likely either to cut yourself on something stuck to his coat or cover your hands in muck and shit which was always stuck to his coat.

So I reluctantly agreed to go up to her mothers with her after asking why her young brother Rob couldn't walk the smelly dog. Rob was in his sister's house and wasn't allowed to have a key so he couldn't go home until his Ma picked him up from his sister's which was on her way home.

It was a windy and dark night and the walk up Shields Road wasn't that easy, so by the time we got to her Ma's house, her Ma's haunted house, remember. I wasn't best pleased at having to walk up three flights of stairs then some more stairs inside the house take the mongrel for a walk before I could go home and get to bed, being half cut didn't help either. We both went up to the house, me moaning at every step and Patricia telling me to shut up at every second step. When we opened the front door to her Ma's house, Shep was sitting right behind it whining and as we pushed the door back he stood and urinated and whined as if afraid.

It was the strangest thing I had never seen a dog urinate before without cocking its leg, but he did. He just stood there cowering and urinated at the bottom of the stairs leading up into the attic flat. Patricia looked at me quite fearfully "Do you think there is somebody up there" she asked.

"No way" I said "But there's only one way to find out" and I ran up the stairs two at a time. When, I opened the living room door my heart stopped beating and my eyes bugged out of my head. Patricia who was behind me seen me stop dead in my tracks and got scared.

"What is it Danny? Is there somebody in there Danny" she stopped about three stairs from the top and added "Danny don't try to frighten me, this isn't funny. Is there somebody in there what is it you can see tell me or I'm going straight back down the stair. Tell me!" she shouted.

"Come and see" I said holding out my hand and taking hers.

She looked and had the same reaction as me, she held her hands up to her mouth in shock and said "Oh my god, look at that Danny" Everything, every single solitary thing in the room was upside down. The sofa, the two chairs, the coffee table. The loose leaf dining table in the corner, as well as the four chairs around it. The fire surround wasn't but it was still attached to the wall. All of the ornaments the length of the mantelpiece were. The pictures on all four walls were hanging upside down. Not a single thing was either broken or out of place, just upside down. Patricia screamed and said we need to get out of here. I disagreed, I was fascinated. I stood the couch the right way up and told Patricia to sit down I wanted to see if anything else was going to happen. She refused she said she was too frightened and was going to sit on the stairs at the bottom of her Ma's close and wait for her. I said I was staying right where I was.

Nothing else happened, or if it did I didn't see it because I fell asleep on the couch and was still sleeping when Patricia her Ma and her brother Rob came upstairs about an hour later. They woke me up, I accused Rob of having a secret key and of doing all this while we were all out, he denied it strenuously. Both Patricia and her Ma said that Shep's actions proved something weird was happening, he had never before did his toilet in the house, ever. I had to admit, even if only to myself, and not to them, seeing the dog standing shivering and urinating was the strangest thing and still gives me goose bumps when I remember it. I still don't know what happened that night. If Rob did it and caught me with a practical joke, well done him, it was brilliant.

It was the last incident in that house that any of us either seen or heard of, because about a month later, Charlie and Iris got offered a house in the high rise flats in the Gorbals and they took it because it was very near Iris' Ma's house. When they moved out of the house next door to us Patricia's Ma and her wee brother Rob moved in. Out of the frying pan and into the fire was my first thought. It wasn't that bad at first because it meant Patricia only had to nip next door when she wanted a cup of tea with her Ma. Since she never worked during the day only at night it also meant they could keep each other company and since I was working all day it didn't matter to me at all really.

One down side was that whenever any do it yourself was required I was right next door and normally free and available. Although to be fair Patricia's ma lost a bit of trust in me when I attached some kitchen units to a wall for her, only for them to fall off a day later not only smashing most of her crockery but also giving her sister's boy Alan Richard a nasty bump on the head.

Naturally it was Alan's fault he was a clumsy wee oaf at the best of times, he had obviously been swinging on one of the doors or something. When Patricia's Ma said that she was there when Alan was just standing beside the cabinets and they fell off the wall on top of him, I didn't believe her. She was just trying to blame me, to be fair it wasn't the first or last time things fell off walls after I put them up. The walls in these old tenements were shocking to tell the truth.

In June of nineteen eighty one, I got some bad news. The job at Cameron Toll was over and my Da's firm only had enough work for the time served scaffolder's on the books. My Da wanted to keep me on and let me learn the trade but it wouldn't have been fair to his other men who had wives and kids to feed and rent to pay. And to be perfectly honest, it really wasn't a great job for me, I was scared of heights, which I thought I had hidden fairly well. But when I revealed it to My Da after he paid me off, he burst out laughing. He along with everyone else on the site had been well aware of how scared I was every time I had to go more than six feet off the ground.

Nobody ever mentioned it not even my brothers because they thought I was brave for even being there although Donnie did say to me once that he knew what scaffolding poles I had been holding on to because I held on to them so tight there were dents where my fingers had been. So that was the scaffolding business done for me, I had loved it while it lasted and I met some fantastic characters and gained a new respect, as if I needed it, for my Da Donnie and Dunky. They were the bravest of the brave no type of weather or danger phased them at all, they were always first up on the steel and last to come down. They earned very good money doing what they did particularly when they worked at Sullom Voe and they deserved every penny.

I still had my Saturdays at the bookies and was sure I would find something else, something maybe less dangerous and more likely to use my brain than my brawn. Patricia still had her job at the bingo and could always try to get extra shifts. Charlie came to me with some good news, well good news for him, he had passed his driving test and bought a wee car. Which was fantastic for him and I was chuffed for him, there wasn't much chance of me doing that anytime soon unless I could find a full time job.

In fact the absolute necessity to find a full time job became very important on our first anniversary when we got the letter back from the doctor's with the result of Patricia's pregnancy test.

Patricia and Danny were going to be a mummy and daddy. We were ecstatic, we both felt ready even though I was only nineteen and Patricia was only seventeen. We really wanted a baby and were so happy. We had been lying in bed when the letter dropped through the door and I had sprung up to get it and brought it back into bed. We knew it was from the Doctor and we ripped it open with excitement, after we had absorbed the news, I wanted to celebrate the way I wanted to celebrate most things. Patricia laughed, pushed my hands away and said "We don't need to keep practicing Danny we know that it works now"

She was joking of course.

Afterword; Book five see's Danny and Patricia embark on raising a family of their own through dire circumstances, whilst continuing to capture the lives of the rest of the McCallister clan. I look forward to seeing you on the next leg of our journey.

Note; Look out for my books in the shops in early 2015, I have just signed a publishing contract, with Fort Publishing. It's strange to think that what started out as a little bit of fun is now blossoming into something that has genuinely captured people's interest. I am extremely surprised and delighted and thank you again.

Printed in Great Britain
by Amazon

62730812R00092